HUNTING FOR WHALES

By
MICHAEL J. MCHUGH

GREAT LIGHT PUBLICATIONS
PALATINE, ILLINOIS

Hunting for Whales
Copyright © 2011 – Michael J. McHugh

All rights reserved. No part of this book may be reproduced or transmitted in any form or by any means, electronic or mechanical, without the written permission of the publisher. Brief quotations embodied in articles or reviews are permitted.

Written by Michael J. McHugh
Text reviewed by Karla McHugh
Cover painting by Clifford W. Ashley
Cover and text designed by Robert Fine
Title page image by Chris Ellithorpe
Harpoon illustration by Hannah McHugh
Text illustrations by Clifford W. Ashley appear on pages iv, 15, 30, 41, 65, 85, 96, 116, 119, & 130
Text photo in chapter 14 copyright Designpics, Inc. (Permission granted)
Song Credits: The song text that appears in chapter ten entitled, *Carlingford*, is copyrighted by Mr. Tommy Makem.

Image credits: Grateful acknowledgement is given to Dover Publications for use of their copyrighted images which appear on pages 37, 49, 58, 63, 76, & 92

A previous version of this book was released by Christian Liberty Press under the title of *Fighting With Whales* in 2002, before they permitted the rights for this work to revert back to the author in 2011.

A publication of
Great Light Publications
422 S. Williams Ave.
Palatine, IL 60074
www.greatlightpublications.com

ISBN 978-0-9822848-7-2

Printed In the United States of America

Dedication & Acknowledgement

This book is dedicated to the famous nineteenth century author and novelist R. M. Ballantyne. His classic whaling book entitled, *Fighting the Whales*, helped to inspire and shape several chapters of the book you are about to read.

IV HUNTING FOR WHALES

Table of Contents

Introduction vii

Chapter 1
Memories of My Youth 1

Chapter 2
A Friendship Begun 5

Chapter 3
An Offer from Captain Flynn 13

Chapter 4
The Seaman's Bethel 21

Chapter 5
Under Sail at Last 29

Chapter 6
There She Blows! 39

Chapter 7
A Floating Butcher Shop 51

Chapter 8
Oil and Trouble 61

Chapter 9
Searching for Water 73

Chapter 10
Big Jack, the Fighting Bull 81

Chapter 11
Death on the High Seas 95

Chapter 12
A New Creature in Christ 107

Chapter 13
A Gam Brings News from Home 119

Chapter 14
Home at Last 127

Chapter 15
Old Glory and New Dreams 137

Bibliography 141

HUNTING FOR WHALES

—INTRODUCTION—

It took a great deal of determination and courage to set out on a whaling voyage in the nineteenth century. Most ship owners required crew members to sign on for at least a two-year voyage, and sometimes demanded as long as a four-year commitment.

The anxiety that many men felt as a result of being taken away from their families or friends for extended periods, was also punctuated by significant periods of utter boredom, when the seas were quiet and the whales were scarce. If the difficulties associated with leaving loved ones and dealing with boredom did not crush you emotionally, then the routine demands of being part of a crew of whaling men was often enough to break you physically. A ceaseless array of tedious watches and hard labor amidst the scorching sun or stormy gale was the common lot of whaling men. Perhaps the greatest threat to life and limb, however, came during the actual act of hunting and processing the whales themselves; unless, of course, you factor in the food that sailors were expected to eat, which was often spoiled or rancid.

All in all, it should not be surprising to discover that most sailors only shipped out on one long whaling voyage during their career. A few hearty men, however, managed to find a way to love this strenuous life, and stayed at sea over the long haul. Some of these men began their whaling careers as cabin boys, and eventually worked their way up to the point where they became captains.

The story you are about to read is a fascinating account of two young men, from very different backgrounds, who experience the adventure of whaling during the mid-nineteenth century. It is a story not only of high sea adventure and hardship, but also of friendship, love, and God's redeeming grace.

Prior to the Civil War in the United States, most Americans living on the eastern seaboard, particularly in New England, considered whaling a very important business enterprise. During these bygone days, the American people relied greatly upon the whaling industry to supply them with useful products, such as whale oil and whalebone. Towns such as New Bedford, Mystic, and Nantucket became prosperous as a result of the popularity of such products.

In modern American society, few people understand why men risked their lives and endured long periods of loneliness simply to hunt for whales. It is the hope of the author, that readers of this book will be able to appreciate the daring exploits of whalemen, and to rightly esteem their accomplishments. May your respect for whales and whaling men grow as you consider what it was like to come face-to- face with a monstrous creature, armed only with an iron spear and Yankee courage.

Michael J. McHugh
Palatine, Illinois
2011

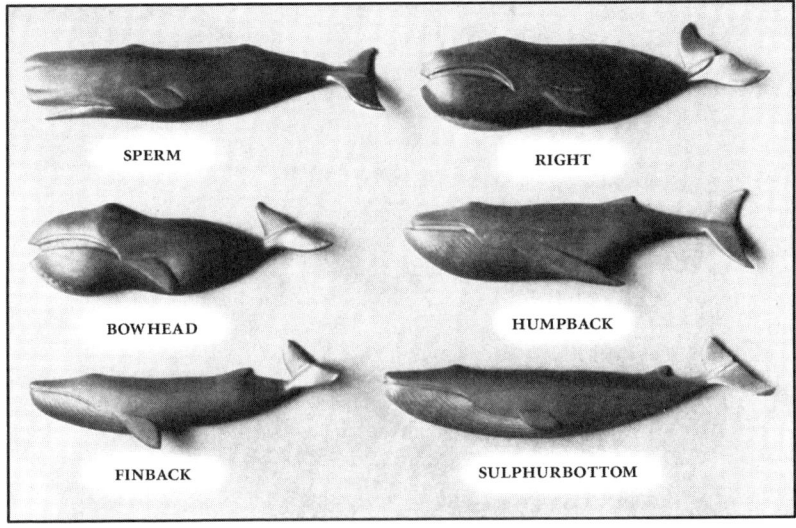

MODELS OF SIX WHALES MADE BY MR. FRANK WOOD

East coast whaling ports of the 1850's
From: The Whalemen's Shipping List, published by the National Marine Digital Library.

Chapter 1
Memories of My Youth

A dense fog rose slowly from the cobblestones of old New Bedford town. It was early in the spring of 1902, and my bones still ached from the dampness and cold.

As I walked slowly on, I began to view the wharf and smell the lingering aroma of rotting canvas and wood. Ninety paces ahead, I could see the tall skeletons of old ships, looking like something out of an elephant graveyard.

Many things had changed in the tiny New England town of New Bedford since the collapse of the whaling industry; but, as an old man, I could still comfort myself in the knowledge that the innkeeper still knew my name. After a long walk, I finally approached the familiar door which led into the Whaler's Inn. Moments later, much to my delight, a plump and seasoned innkeeper bellowed out my name.

"For the love of big whales, if it isn't old Jim Surrey!" spouted the proprietor of the dimly lit establishment. "What brings you in from the cold, my friend? Have you a taste for a bowl of chowder this fine day?"

"No, No," I responded. "Staying away from your chowder has caused me to live into old age. My hope is to meet with my old shipmate, Timothy Dronner, and to rekindle our friendship."

"Well, if you can't have a warm stomach this day, may ye have a heartwarming gam with your friend," replied the good-natured innkeeper.

As I moved deeper into the confines of the inn, a corner booth graced with an oil lamp came before me. Sitting down, I quickly set aside my cap and cane and ordered up a hot drink. Before long, I found myself signaling to the innkeeper for another drink to be brought as I recognized the voice of an old friend coming closer to my ears.

"Hallo, Master Jim!" asserted the bright-eyed visitor named Timothy Dronner. "I hardly thought to see ye out this day considering the cold and damp."

"My old bones never could tell me what to do with my time mate. We seldom find the time for a gam, dear friend, so I am here even though me bones are talking kinda loud these days. Sit down, then, sit down before ye fall down."

"Jim, can it truly be that we shipped out on our first voyage almost sixty years ago?" asked Timothy as he began to puff on his long-necked pipe.

"Pretty nearly so, my friend, we were but mere lads and as green as cucumbers," I responded. "Even after all these years since we have hung up our oilskins, I still can't get used to seeing New Bedford town so still and quiet. Time was when every part of town was bursting with activity."

"I know what you mean," said Timothy quickly. "I can still see Captain Flynn strolling down the wharf, top hat and all."

"It's hard to keep from thinking about the days of our youth, old friend," I added, as I began to stare into a nearby fireplace. "It all seems like a wild dream, and, at the rate our memories are fading, even the dream may soon be gone."

"We must not let the story of whaling men be capsized and lost, shipmate," said the concerned old sailor named Timothy as he turned to the crowd gathered at the inn.

Moments later, this grey-haired salt of the sea boldly stood up and addressed the curious onlookers. "Dear people of New Bedford, my name is Timothy Dronner, and I ask thee to gather round and lend an ear to my friend and former shipmate, Jim Surrey. He has a tale worth telling about the great days of sail and of the men who fought big whales. Fill your glasses then, and listen to my friend spin a story worth passing on to your children and grandchildren."

Slowly, people began to position themselves close to the heavy wooden table where I sat, in utter silence, still taken aback by the boldness of my friend's speech. A short time later, a small group of townspeople sat staring at me as I reluctantly resigned myself to the task of telling the story of my adventures as a whaling man.

A prolonged hush fell over the Whaler's Inn as I slowly began to explain how I was first led to become a whale hunter. Amidst the clanking of glasses and shuffling of chairs, I started to take on the role of an old storyteller by lifting up my gravelly voice and beginning a voyage of words.

For I've a husband out at sea
Afloat on feeble planks of wood;
He does not know what fear may be;
I would have told him if I could.

Christina Rossetti
(1830–1894)

Chapter 2
A Friendship Begun

About sixty years ago, I lived with my mother in the nearby town of Fairhaven. Many is the time that I would look across the Acushnet River toward New Bedford and watch the world's greatest whaling port receive another heavily laden vessel. Even now, if I close my eyes, I can smell the sweet odor flowing from the hundreds of barrels of whale oil that used to routinely sit on the waterfront docks of New Bedford.

As a young lad, I would listen as my mother would tell of the day that my dear father shipped out on a three-year voyage to the Azores in search of seals and whale. Like many men before him, my father never returned alive. The word that came to my mother from the ship's captain, was that he took sick on the voyage out and died. Being nowhere close to land, they were forced to bury him at sea.

Many were the tears that flowed down my mother's cheeks as she labored in her spirit to accept the Almighty's will. The passing of the head of our home, however, also meant that we would no longer have any meaningful source of income for our household. The first winter after my father's death, we did receive some assistance when my mother was given the money that my father had earned from the share he had in his final voyage. This payment of the so-called "part" of the voyage lasted but a few months, however, and then we hit the hard times.

My widow mother soon began to work in order to provide for our daily needs of food and shelter after the money was gone. Even now, I can recall the many times when her toilsome labor was rewarded with only a bundle full of wool, or perhaps with a pail of milk or a fish. Funny though, I don't recall her ever complaining about her lot.

As I grew older, it became necessary for me to help my mother as she began to work for the wealthy class of merchants and ship owners that inhabited the waterfront mansions. Each week, my mother and I would take in laundry and do odd jobs of every sort in order to make ends meet. Life was often hard without Father, but we stayed too busy to feel sorry for ourselves, and managed to make a living by the skin of our teeth.

In my youth, it seemed as though everyone worked in the business of whaling in some manner. The shopkeepers in town serviced the needs of crews and ships alike. The cooper's shops were hard pressed to keep up with the demand for suitable barrels, and the carpenters and riggers seldom lacked employment. Even boys were expected to run errands, or to help out the ship owners where and when they could.

In spite of all this hustle and bustle, however, boys like myself still managed to have plenty of time to dream and play. Every boy dreamed of being the captain of an ivory-trimmed bark, or at least an officer of some kind. Whenever time permitted, my friends and I would gather around the blacksmith's shop and listen to whalers tell of their adventures on the high seas. Before long, our heads became so filled with whaling stories, that we would spend hours arguing with each other about which whale was the biggest or most fierce.

One day in early March, in the year of our Lord 1846, as I was running an errand for my mother, I heard a loud noise coming from the direction of the blacksmith's shop. Running on, I saw two young boys fighting with each other. The one lad held a knife in his hand and the other a wooden stick. Almost without thinking, I proceeded to pick up a large apple from a nearby fruit stand and hurl it at the boy who held the knife. My aim was unusually good that day, and I was able to hit the knife-wielding lad square on the side of his head. Moments later, this young man found himself lying dazed on the street in front of the blacksmith's shop.

A stout man with big arms and a short temper walked over to where the lad was lying, and picked up his knife. This gentleman was the best known blacksmith in town, and he rarely spoke without good reason. You had better believe, then, that everyone who was in earshot listened carefully as he spoke.

"I won't tolerate any more trouble around my place!" shouted the angry shopkeeper. "If ye need to fuss and quarrel, lads, go settle your disputes in front of someone else's establishment."

Although the boy with the wooden stick seemed content enough with the declaration of the blacksmith, the lad on the ground appeared to receive the news with considerably less glee, for the shopkeeper proceeded to toss a bucket of cold water upon him.

The crowd on the street, including myself, thought the whole scene was quite amusing. After I regained my composure, I walked over to the lad who, moments before, had been staring down the length of a knife blade.

"Many thanks, stranger," said the grateful young man. "My name is Timothy Dronner, but my friends call me Tim. What be your name?"

"The name is Jim Surrey. What brings you into town this day, besides fighting? You strike me as a greenhorn from the country!"

"Where I come from is none of your business, and as for fighting, well, let's just say that I've had enough fighting for one day. I came to this town to find work as a whaler. I have always dreamed of catching big fish," responded the lad, confidently.

"Well enough, stranger. But how do you hope to become a whaleman when you do not as yet know that whales are mammals, not fish? Besides, you are not yet eighteen, as near as I can tell."

"I'll sort that out in good time, Jim. To tell you the truth, I'm more concerned about where my next meal will come from. Do you have any more large apples that I could utilize for eating rather than throwing?"

"I'm afraid not," I chuckled. "Perhaps you would like to follow me home to see what's left in my mother's cupboard?"

"If you're inviting me to your home, then I ain't too proud to follow," said the thankful stranger.

As the crowd finally dispersed, the two of us walked slowly toward my mother's humble dwelling on the other side of the bay. After several minutes, I asked my new found companion how he was planning to eat without money or employment.

"Well, I guess I underestimated the difficulties," Tim responded. "I had lately determined that I would set to begging for my food, but I must admit that I had no stomach for a life built around handouts."

The young stranger went on to explain how he had offered his services to several shop owners in New Bedford in a clumsy manner with no success. His shame was lessened to some degree only because he knew that he was willing to work, if only someone would give him the opportunity.

As my new companion and I traveled on, we stopped at a local dry goods shop to pick up a few things for my darling mother. At this spot, I purchased a pound of tea, flour, sugar, and a crock of butter. As we were about to leave the store, I also decided to procure a few hard biscuits and some honey as snacks for the remaining trip home.

In the space of just under an hour after we left the dry goods shop, young Tim and I reached our home. My mother was standing in the kitchen when we arrived, cutting up the last scraps of food that we had to our name. The walk home near the cool water had given both of us a slight chill, so I was glad to see that she had built a hearty fire in the fireplace, and filled the tea kettle while I was gone.

"We have a guest, Mother," I remarked, in an effort to get her attention.

"I do have spectacles my dear boy, but I am not blind," opened my mother as she looked in our direction.

"Yes, well, hello madam," began the unemployed visitor in an awkward fashion. "Please don't be put off with my coming at dinner time; I can assure you that I won't take from your meager stores," added the stranger.

"Our stores may be meager young man," replied the woman as she straightened her shawl, "but I have yet to turn away the honest poor from our table on any account. It is, however, my custom to at least know the name of every person seated around my table. You do have a name, I suppose?" asked the woman of the house.

"Oh, forgive me mother, for neglecting to mention our guest's name. It is Timothy Dronner," said the embarrassed son. "He is new in town, and in search of work."

"Well, such a situation will require a great deal of energy on his part, particularly in these days when work is scarce," she remarked. "A meal or two from our table should be just what he needs to prepare him for the challenges ahead," she added in an effort to be more cheerful.

"Speaking of challenges," asserted the curious guest, "I can't help but ask how a woman of your limited means can manage to keep a house provisioned and still have extra to spare for needy folks like me?"

"Do you really want to know how it is that I can make ends meet, young man?" inquired my mother. "It is by trusting with simple child-like faith in the promises that are contained in that Book," she added, while pointing over to a Bible that sat on a stool near her.

"Many times over the years of my youth I have wished for such a faith as yours," replied the visitor. "Even now, as I consider what my future may hold, I am as nervous as a cat about how things will work out."

"Being a widow for an extended period has helped me to be more trusting of my Maker, and more aware of how much I need Him each day. Yet, more than this, I have discovered that true faith does not come from making wishes, but by believing on the promise of Jesus Christ who said, 'I shall never leave you, nor forsake you.' I expect to have my basic needs met today, because I know that my son will be diligent in helping to care for me, and that God will do the rest."

My new friend did not seem to know how to respond to my mother's words, and so he simply smiled and began to stare at her with a look of admiration. Moments later, I decided to ask my astonished guest if he would like to help me unpack the groceries and set the table. Not surprisingly, he was more than pleased to honor my request.

Shortly after dinner was finished, we all sat in front of the fire and enjoyed a cup of tea, punctuated by small talk. Before long, in spite of my efforts to discourage him, Tim began speaking to us about the plans that he had to sign on a whaling ship bound for the South Seas.

"I long for adventure and a chance to make a living on the sea," insisted our self-assured visitor.

"Dying is a hard way to make a living," responded my mother in a firm yet quiet manner. "Many is the man who looked for the sea to bring him his fortune, only to find incredible hardships and a watery grave. My own husband lies at the bottom of the ocean even now."

"I regret your husband's fate, dear woman," replied the young man soberly. "Yet I hasten to say that in hard times like these, there are few options open to a young man such as myself, seeing that my learning is no good. It's either the mines or the mill back home, for I was never cut out to be a farmer like my father."

"And just how do you plan on getting hired on a whaling vessel with no experience, and nobody to sponsor your application?" questioned my widow mother.

"As I have already told your generous son, my dear lady, I will sort this out in good time. If you will but pray for me, madam, I am sure that something proper will come my way in the Lord's good time."

"Very well, then," she concluded. "We will offer you our prayers and our food this fine evening. By the way, it appears as though the evening hours are far spent. Will you be staying the night then, Mr. Dronner?"

"If you are willing, then I will be staying," said the grateful visitor.

"James, dear," said my mother. "Your new friend will be staying the night. Please get the bedroll down from the attic for our weary guest to sleep upon."

After the dishes were cleaned, my mother soon fell asleep upon the couch next to the fireplace. Tim Dronner and I spoke of many things that night before our eyelids became too heavy. More often than not, however, the topic eventually turned back to whaling.

"Why don't we look for a ship that would suit us both, Master Jim? New Bedford has plenty of tall ships."

"Why don't you just drop all this talk about whaling, Tim, once and for all? How many times do I have to tell you that I have no interest in joining you on some absurd voyage to fight whales!"

"The dream of adventure on the high seas is in my head to stay, Jim," he responded. "Seeing how we have become fast friends, it is only natural that I would want you to join me in the fun. Don't answer now, Jim, sleep on it and we can talk again in the morning."

Chapter 3
An Offer from Captain Flynn

The next morning dawned brightly as I awoke to the sound of seagulls flying nearby. My new friend, Tim, and my mother were putting something together for breakfast in the kitchen. As I walked in, the two were jabbering as if they had known each other for years.

"What are you two talking about?" I asked

"Wouldn't you like to know," responded my mother slyly.

"I think I can guess, dear woman," was my reply. "Our old friend Tim here has been filling your head with wild stories about how he and I are bound to be shipmates on a Yankee whaler."

"How would it be that you could know such things," asked my mother. "You never used to be able to listen through walls."

Turning my attention to the overzealous visitor, I quipped, "Give up this foolishness, lad. You are only bound to upset my mother's fragile constitution. Besides, we had best turn our attention to the more urgent need of finding you employment. Even whalemen need money to live on, and you have the need to buy a load of gear before you think about setting foot on a bark."

"Very well," agreed the slender country boy, reluctantly.

After completing a brief but satisfying breakfast, Tim and I hitched a ride on a horse drawn wagon that was headed for town. As the minutes passed, we discussed how and where we would try to find him work.

"How do you earn a living?" asked Tim.

"For years now," I answered, "I have found work doing odd jobs for almost every shopkeeper in town. If you have a mind for work and a strong back, someone will at least give you day wages running errands or working on the wharfs unloading cargo."

Tim smiled widely for several moments, and then, amidst chuckles, stated that he was not so sure if he wanted to work for the blacksmith.

"He is a might too stern for my liking," concluded Tim.

"His bark is worse than his bite," I added with a smile. "Besides, he is not the only blacksmith in New Bedford."

A few minutes later, the small wagon we were riding in came to an abrupt halt at the outskirts of town.

"This is where ye lads must depart," shouted the driver. "I hope you earn a few dollars for your sweat this day."

As we jumped from the back of the wagon to the cobblestone street below, Tim tossed the driver a hard biscuit, and then put his floppy hat on more securely.

"Now where?" asked Tim.

"Straight ahead to the wharf," I suggested. "Just follow the gulls. Two vessels are due in today, so we should be able to find some kind of work."

Several minutes passed before we reached the vicinity of the wharf. As predicted, the entire area around the docks was a beehive of activity. As I knew the routine, I took the initiative to inquire with the manager of the docks about the availability of work.

The dock foreman was a wiry chap by the name of Terry. He sported a large mustache and a huge scar on the side of his face. The scar was a memento from his younger days as a pirate, I was told.

"Who is it that ye brought with you, Jim boy?" inquired the scarred man.

"My friend's name is Timothy, Timothy Dronner sir," I answered.

An Offer from Captain Flynn

"Can he work, Jim?" questioned the foreman. "He looks much too pretty to be a working man. We don't hire no greenhorns, Jim boy."

"I can work well enough," said Tim. "Give me a chance to prove myself."

"He speaks pretty bold for a lad with no references," barked the foreman. "Oh, well, I am in a tight spot today so I will try him out for size just this once."

Something like a smile broke out on Tim's face as he followed the dock manager over to where his first job was to begin.

As the sun rose higher in the sky, Tim and I unloaded cargo of every sort. The afternoon's work dragged on as we endured the incessant rambling of the foreman who yelled, "Put your backs into it, boys!" at least a hundred times. The best part of the day, by far, was the lunch break. We were permitted to eat our fish and chips in relative peace, as we took turns feeding the seagulls with our scraps.

Strange smells also intruded themselves upon us during our labors on the wharf next to Water Street. Among the more memorable smells was the scent of whale oil mixed with dried fish. My friend, Tim, had a particularly difficult time handling the peculiar and sometimes overpowering odors. More than once, my friend from the country seemed to turn a strange shade of green as he struggled to adapt to the rude smells.

A man had to work hard to earn two dollars a day in the 1840s, but we were glad to have the work just the same. Our day work down at the wharf lasted six days, before the foreman informed us that he had run short of work. This unwelcome news meant that my friend and I were, once again, in search of employment. We eventually found work running errands for the local baker, which involved transporting barrels of bread from his shop to the holds of several vessels being outfitted for their eventual voyage.

I still remember how it felt when we first set foot on a whale ship. All was clean and tidy on board as a rule, and the sheer size of the masts and yardarm were enough to impress most persons our age. The wealthier ship owners had their whaling vessels trimmed with fixtures made of brass or whalebone. Some of the whalers that had captured whales in previous voyages also utilized the jawbones of their victims to form a portion of the rudder shafts or helms.

Late one day, as we were finishing up a delivery of hardtack to a three masted schooner, we received an important message from the baker. His message told us of an urgent delivery that needed to be made before nightfall.

The most famous captain in New Bedford town, Captain Argus Flynn, was set to sail within a fortnight, and he was anxious to get his supplies safely stored in his ship's hold. Little did we know how our lives would change as a result of a simple delivery of hard biscuits to a whaling bark.

Captain Flynn's vessel, the *Landsman*, was well known to the citizens of New Bedford, so we had little trouble finding his ship. As the cart we were driving pulled alongside the ivory-trimmed *Landsman*, a skinny man in a broad-rimmed hat called to us saying; "Ahoy there, what's your business, lads?"

We informed the strange looking sailor of our mission, and he quickly motioned for us to haul our cargo up the gangplank, and then disappeared. Moments later, we began to push ten barrels of bread onto the main deck of the *Landsman* with no assistance of any kind. All during this process, much to our surprise, we saw nary a soul. We suspected that the man who greeted us had gone below deck, and that we were free to go.

We no sooner turned around, however, before we were staring directly at none other than Captain Flynn himself.

"Well, well, what brings ye landlubbers aboard my ship?" questioned the captain. "Has the baker finally gotten round to making good on my order of hardtack?"

"Yes, sir," I responded. "Ten barrels, just as you ordered, Captain."

"How would you like to earn an extra half dollar in silver this fine evening?" asked Captain Flynn.

Tim responded, "We ain't afraid of hard work, and anyways, we could sure use the extra pay, for we're fixing to outfit ourselves as whaling men."

"Oh, whalemen, shipmates is it then!" said the captain. "Well, why don't you ambitious lads show me what you're made of by stowing these here barrels below deck, as well as the others over yonder."

As soon as he was finished speaking, the captain excused himself, and we set to work clearing the deck of cargo and storing it in the hold below. Several minutes later, after we had finished our main task, the first mate directed us to help him stow surplus canvas in a special place in the forecastle of the *Landsman*.

"She sure is a fine ship," said Tim admiringly, as we prepared to leave.

Captain Flynn had overheard my friend Tim and said, "I can see you are a good judge of vessels, lad, even if you are a mite bit green. Here be your half dollar."

"Thank you, sir," said I. "Will you be needin' anything else, Captain, before we shove off?"

"No more to do at this hour," said the captain slowly as he stroked his cropped beard. "All I ask is that you help spread the word that the *Landsman* needs several new mates, for five of my regular crew have taken sick of late and likely will be unfit to sail."

"Might we qualify as shipmates, sir?" said Tim impulsively.

"What do you mean by we, friend? I don't recall Jim Surrey ever committing to be a whaler," said I.

"Hold onto your hats, lads," recommended Captain Flynn. "I know you both are hard working souls, but what else can ye do besides stow cargo? Can either of ye sing and hold to a cadence? Can ye pull teeth or set an arm, or do anything useful as a mate?"

"Well, sir, I mean, Captain," mumbled Tim. "My father taught me many things on the farm, including how to pull the teeth of animals, and how to set the broken leg of a sheep."

"Excellent!" yelled the captain. "You will do nicely as our ship's doctor. Now what about your reluctant shipmate?"

"My reluctance to sign on, sir, has to do with the death of my father these three years ago," I remarked. "Even now, my dear widowed mother is barely making it by with my help. As for singing, my father was a whaler and a hearty singer, and he taught me all the songs of the chanteyman."

"My regrets, son, on the loss of your father, but may you not do your mother more financial good by earning profits as a whaleman rather than an errand boy?"

"Perhaps," said I. "But I doubt that I would do my mother any service by leaving her alone for three years."

"Rest easy, son, for my ship is outward bound for only a two-year voyage," added the captain. "Furthermore, you can perhaps find someone to care for your mother in your absence. Think on it well, lad, and let me know your decision soon."

As Tim and I walked down the gangplank to the waiting horse and cart, we barely said a word. Each of us was lost in his own thoughts. Finally, after a minute or two, Tim asked; "Am I dreaming, or did Captain Argus Flynn just hire me on as a mate and ship's doctor?"

"I'm afraid so," I responded. "It should be a wild adventure for you and for your patients, doctor."

"Jim, don't think for a moment that I would go to sea without you. If you refuse to go, then my answer to the captain will also be 'no'."

Chapter 4
The Seaman's Bethel

The thought of seeking approval from my widow mother for a two-year voyage, was only slightly less distasteful than the notion of continuing on in the role of an errand boy indefinitely.

Several days had already gone by, however, since I spoke with Captain Flynn and time was growing short. Therefore, I determined to approach my mother and let her know my desires. At midweek, I decided to come home early in order to be able to speak with her.

"Good evening, Mother," was my greeting.

"My word, is it evening already, Son, or has my sense of time gone away?" she responded.

"Your senses are still with you, Mother. I decided to come home early so we could talk."

"What's on your mind, Son? You look perplexed."

"I am," said I. "Captain Argus Flynn has asked Timothy and me to sign on his crew for a two-year voyage. He says that it is just the break a young man like me needs."

"Oh, I see," responded my mother softly. "And what, if I may ask, will happen with me?"

"That's why I am perplexed, Mother," I said frankly.

"When I don't know how to figure out things, I call on Reverend Carlson down at the Seaman's Bethel for counsel," stated my mother. "Why don't you pay him a visit this very night?"

"I haven't been very regular at services lately, Mother, with my long hours at work. Do you think he will see me?"

"Of course, my boy. Now, go get washed up, and see if you can borrow the neighbor's horse for your ride to New Bedford."

Thanks to the generosity of our next-door neighbor, I was soon riding a swift horse in the direction of the parson who lived atop Johnnycake Hill.

The Seaman's Bethel had been the primary church for whale men in New Bedford town since my father was in britches. Any sailor with an ounce of spiritual concern would pay a visit to the Bethel prior to departing on a voyage, so as to make peace with his Maker. The church building itself, which had held many a whaler's wedding and funeral, was decorated with plaques that commemorated the voyages and deaths of many sailors.

As I began to approach the vicinity of the church, I passed numerous small shops and boarding houses. Moving down the cobbled streets on horseback was more difficult than I had anticipated, so I decided to dismount and walk the final block to Rev. Carlson's parsonage.

Upon arriving, I knocked on the front door of the tiny dwelling. Moments later, I heard footsteps and was soon standing before the venerable preacher. He invited me into his study after I explained the purpose of my visit, and we set to talking.

"So how is your dear mother these days, James?" inquired the minister.

"Very well, Reverend."

"How can I be of service to you this evening?" he asked.

"I need your advice on a matter that concerns my mother and my career. It all stems from the fact that, only recently, I've been offered a spot on Captain Flynn's crew, and must quickly decide whether to leave my mother to further my career."

"I see," said Rev. Carlson. "And you are wondering whether it is right to place the demands of your vocation above the needs of your widowed mother."

"Yes, I suppose that is what it amounts to, sir."

"Our Lord had a critically important job to do in His capacity as Savior, a work which placed Him in the position of having to leave His beloved mother. Yet, the Scriptures tell us that Christ took the time to ensure that Mary would be well cared for after His departure. As Jesus hung on the cross, He made sure to entrust His mother's care into the hands of John, a trusted friend."

"And you are saying, then, that I should seek to do no less? Is that correct?"

"Yes, precisely, my friend," said the parson.

"Do you have any recommendations for a suitable caretaker for my mother?" I asked.

"Yes, I have but one recommendation, dear lad, me."

"Forgive me, preacher, but I thought I just heard you say that you would care for my mother for the next two years."

"Your hearing is quite intact, James," responded Rev. Carlson, with a smile.

"I—I hardly know what to say except 'Thank you,' and that I will pledge to help you pay for my mother's care upon my return."

"I know you will do what you can out of your limited means, James," Rev. Carlson assured me. "Now, promise me that you will be at the Sunday service before you ship out."

"Very well, Reverend. Thanks again for your help."

We closed our meeting a short time later, as the evening was drawing on fast. As I began my homeward journey, my thoughts quickly centered upon how my mother would react to the unexpected proposal.

Much to my surprise, I soon discovered that my mother was rather at peace with the notion of Rev. Carlson as her temporary guardian. She obviously believed that she would be well looked after, because she knew that the preacher was a man of his word.

When I broke the news to Tim Dronner about my acceptance of Captain Flynn's invitation to join his crew, I thought he would come unglued. Shouts of joy, and something like an Irish jig, quickly sprung forth from us both, much to the amusement of onlookers.

Our momentary glee soon turned more to sober contemplation, however, as we both considered how ill-equipped we were to take to sea. With only three days left before our departure, my shipmate and I decided to pay a visit to the outfitters and clothing shops on Main Street.

Our inexperience forced us to ask the proprietor of the best clothing shop in town what gear he would recommend that whalers purchase. As Tim and I listened carefully, the shop owner gave us our first lesson on seafaring survival.

"Cold, wet, and dirty work it is, boys," began the shopkeeper. "I urge you to obtain two heavy wool sweaters, a good pair of waterproof boots, and above all else a set of oilskins. O yes, and for your sakes, and that of your shipmates, don't forget to bring plenty of soap!"

Within one hour, much to our satisfaction, we had purchased nearly all the gear we needed, and certainly all we could afford. As it turned out, the advice we received was worth its weight in gold, and many times at sea we were thankful to God and the shopkeeper for their help.

The time was fast approaching when we would need to board the *Landsman*, and we soon began to say our good-byes in town and at home. The day before we were to depart was Sunday, the Lord's Day, so I finished the last of my errands on Saturday and prepared to attend the Seaman's Bethel service as promised. Although it took a bit of prodding, I was able to convince Tim Dronner to join me for the worship service on Sunday morning, as well.

The church meeting that Sunday was unusually crowded, as sailors from all over the area were intent on getting right with the Almighty before they began a dangerous voyage. Precisely at eleven o'clock, Rev. Carlson emerged from his study to take the pulpit.

He opened, "Beloved friends and sailors, let us pray. Almighty God, who hears prayers that are offered up in spirit and in truth, unite our hearts in the holy exercise of biblical worship. Permit us to feed upon Your Word and Spirit to the nourishment of our needy souls. Grant that we may enter into your rest, and your peace, this day through Jesus Christ our Lord, Amen."

"For many of you," the preacher continued, "this Lord's day marks your last time of fellowship with us, for you will soon be shipping out and unable to attend sacred worship here for an extended period of time. For at least a few of you, however, this may well be the last time you ever visit the Seaman's Chapel, because you will have tasted death, and been ushered into the presence of your Maker. The question is, shipmates, are you prepared for what the Lord brings into your path? Can you say, with the Apostle Paul, 'For me to live is Christ and to die is gain'?"

"My primary message to you today comes from the book of First Timothy, chapter one. In this passage, Paul the Apostle acknowledges that before Christ took over his life, he was a blasphemer, a persecutor of Christians, and a violent man. All men sailing through the journey of life, like Paul, are sinners and are unworthy of the love and grace of God.

"Beloved friends, have you ever been brought to the place of seeing yourself as Paul saw himself? As one who is totally unfit for heaven? If so, then you have discovered a truth that will lead you to a Rock that is higher than yourself; you will have seen your need for an anchor for your souls. Hope then will be near, as near as the Savior Jesus Christ is to His lost sheep. As David the Psalmist declared in Psalm thirty-four, verse eighteen, 'The Lord is nigh unto them that are of a broken heart; and saveth such as be of a contrite spirit.'

"Will you abandon your proud spirit to receive the free offer of mercy and grace that God's Word offers you today? Will you accept, by faith, the bloody work of Christ on Calvary's cross as the full atonement for your sins?

"Dear ones, you must answer these questions with a willing mind or perish! You must come to God, through the mercy of Christ alone, by faith alone, and by the power of the Holy Spirit alone. Should your hard, stony hearts cast away the words of this Gospel of Christ, mark me well, once you have cast off faith you will surely make shipwreck. This truth is made plain by Paul the Apostle in First Timothy, chapter one.

Beginning in verse fifteen, the Apostle declares: "This is a faithful saying, and worthy of all acceptation, that Christ Jesus came into the world to save sinners; of whom I am chief. Howbeit for this cause I obtained mercy, that in me first Jesus Christ might show forth all longsuffering, for a pattern to them which should hereafter believe on him to life everlasting. Now unto the King eternal, immortal, invisible, the only wise God, be honour and glory for ever and ever. Amen."

Paul the Apostle then concludes his inspired remarks to his co-laborer Timothy with these words of admonition regarding faith: "This charge I commit unto thee, son Timothy, according to the prophecies which went before on thee, that thou by them mightest war a good warfare; Holding faith, and a good conscience; which some having put away concerning faith have made shipwreck: Of whom is Hymenaeus and Alexander;

whom I have delivered unto Satan, that they may learn not to blaspheme."

"Think on these things well, shipmates, and pray for the Lord to grant you the gifts of faith and repentance, without which no one will gain peace and joy in this life, or in the next. Amen."

Rev. Carlson concluded the service with the hymn *Amazing Grace*, which was written by a former sea captain and slave trader, John Newton. After the final hymn, many of the men stayed in the church sanctuary for several minutes, and said the last of their farewells to family and friends.

The following morning, I went early to the ship after a tearful parting with my mother. As it was only the tail end of winter, I was grateful that I had remembered to put on my thickest sweater, for the air was cool. Looking across the docks, I noticed the familiar face of my friend and shipmate, Tim, as he approached.

In keeping with an old custom, we both kneeled down and kissed the ground before making our way on to the *Landsman*. As we approached the gangplank, I turned to my friend and said, "After you, Doctor Dronner, my esteemed colleague."

"Get off it, Jim," moaned my agitated friend as he chased me up the gangplank and onto the ship.

Chapter 5
Under Sail at Last

The breeze quickened as the crew of the *Landsman* made final preparations for getting under way and out of the harbor. Amidst the sound of rattling chains and clanking gears, our strongest men finally succeeded in hoisting the anchor. Before long, our bark began to pass slowly into the current that flowed like a stream out of the harbor. As we proceeded, a bell rang out from our vessel amidships, just as we were about to round the point near Palmer Island bound for the open sea. As the wind began to fill the few sails that we had on our masts, the first mate called out to me.

"Chanteyman, give these hearties something to pull to, a song lad, a song!"

As the men began to work together in the unfurling of more canvas aloft, I opened my mouth and chanted this opening verse of song: "O boats and clothes are all in pawn."

The chorus was then immediately sung in unison by the sailors who were part of the working party, "Go down you blood red roses, go down. Oh, you pinks and posies; Go down you blood red roses, go down."

Then I sang, "For it's round Cape Horn that we must go," before the men chimed in with another verse from the chorus.

And then my chantey continued, "For that is where them whale fish blow."

On and on my chantey song went, as I added one new verse at a time, while the response of the laboring sailors was always to repeat the words of the simple chorus in unison.

The job of the chanteyman was, more than anything, to keep the morale of the men high as they frequently faced difficult and demanding physical labor. As even a landlover can recognize, hard tasks seem a bit lighter and more pleasant when they are done to music, for tunes help us to forget our troubles.

As our bark continued to cut through the water, I heard the captain yell to the first mate: "Put on every inch of canvas she will hold. Get more men in the rigging!"

As men sprang aloft to do the captain's will, the *Landsman* slowly picked up speed as its sails began to unfurl. In what

seemed like only a few moments, the tiny buildings of New Bedford town began to fade, and then completely disappeared from view. At this point, it was clear to every soul on board that we were finally engaged in an adventure on the high seas, with all of its great expectations.

The initial exuberance of sailors such as myself quickly faded, however, as the rolling waves of the ocean began to play havoc with my stomach. These opening days at sea made me so miserable, that I began to wonder if my skin was going to turn a permanent shade of green. After a few days, however, I began to feel considerably better; or as the seasoned sailors put it, to 'get my sea legs about me.'

As things turned out, it was a good thing that I became accustomed to the rolling of the ship, for one of my first regular duties was to act as a lookout. Most of the men on board despised having to climb the rigging to the tiny platform or "crow's nest" that protruded from the masthead in order to function as a lookout. For one thing, sailors commonly regarded the duty of a lookout as tedious and dangerous, even though large metal hoops surrounded the place at the top of the masthead where one would be stationed. In spite of the dangers involved and some occasional boredom, I truly learned to love this duty, particularly when the weather was calm. I grew to appreciate the hours I could spend far above the hustle and noise of the *Landsman*, for this afforded me the unfettered opportunity to contemplate my life in relative peace.

I well remember, in the early part of our voyage, how I spent many pleasant hours watching the blue horizon and thinking about the new direction that my life had taken. At moments like these, as the wind blew softly upon my cheeks, my thoughts would often turn to the counsel that I received from Rev. Carlson shortly before my journey began. He urged me to '…keep yourself in the study of God's Word, Jim, and as much as possible, away from evil companions.'

As I sat in the solitude of my tiny perch far above deck, it did not seem very difficult to stay on the straight and narrow. Once I climbed down to the main deck and began to rub shoulders with my other shipmates, however, the business of living for God suddenly became more challenging. Still, I had much for which to be grateful, for some of my fellow shipmates professed Christ, and most were a rather even-tempered lot as a rule.

Our first weeks at sea went rather smoothly, as the men became accustomed to working with the captain and the ship. In between seasons of hard work and silly games or customs, I found that there was general boredom on board. I tried my best, therefore, to use my talents as a man of music to help lift the spirits of the men and keep them from becoming discouraged.

Although Captain Flynn could be a hard and demanding skipper at times, at least in the early stages of our voyage, he would commonly leave the men to do as they liked when they were not on duty. As long as his crew refrained from fighting or destructive behavior, the captain was inclined to spend most of his time in his cabin studying charts or visiting with the other officers.

As I learned later in our voyage, not every skipper of a whaling vessel has the nerve to give his men as much liberty as we initially received. One reason for this, stems from the fact that the crew on a whaler was often rather large compared to other merchant ships. Large numbers of men were needed on board a whaling bark to handle the catching and processing of the whales that were harvested from the sea. The *Landsman*, for instance, had a crew of three mates or officers, in addition to the captain. It also had four harpooners, a carpenter who did general carpentry as well as barrel-making, a blacksmith, a cook, a steward, three sail makers, a cabin boy, and twenty seamen.

To keep from going insane, many of my shipmates had a hobby or craft that they practiced in their spare time. The most popular hobby on the *Landsman*, as it was on most whalers, involved the carving of images or decorations on to the face of the bones or teeth of whales. This craft, which is truly an art form, is called "scrimshaw." Sailors would work hour after hour sitting and scratching on the surface of whale bones, while they patiently filled in their designs with black ink.

Under Sail at Last

Virtually all of the aspects of life on a whaling bark were subject to a very predictable routine, which was part of the reason why men that were living under such conditions were so subject to becoming melancholy. Even the time and place for our meals was strictly regimented. Our meal or mess times began at seven in the morning, and then continued with the midday meal at noon, with supper around sunset at 5:30 P.M.

The captain and officers commonly ate at a table near the captain's quarters, while we common sailors were fed from large pots of food that were brought from the galley, and served to us in the forecastle on small metal pans. Most of our meals consisted of pork and beans, or some kind of stew or soup that was supplemented with whatever we could catch from the sea. Each meal also had some kind of potato dish, and a piece of hard, unleavened bread known as 'hard-tack.' Our drink was commonly tea or a watered down coffee, sweetened with black molasses. On special occasions, however, a crude form of rum or ale known as 'grog' was made available to those who were so inclined.

Favorable winds blew us gracefully onward toward our first destination in the South Atlantic. As the days continued to pass, we soon found ourselves crossing over the equator, or as we sailors call it, "the line." As we crossed the line, the seasoned crewmembers enforced the old and silly custom of shaving the heads of all of those who had never sailed over the equator. Needless to say, Tim and I wore caps quite regularly for several days, as our mates were poor barbers indeed!

It was already well into the month of May, and although our voyage out was relatively trouble free, we were all getting rather anxious to spot our first whale. When the expectation for battle or adventure begins to stir in a whaleman's veins, the old-timers refer to it as the time when his "blood is up." At last, we arrived at our hunting grounds just north and east of Cape Horn, but our blood remained quite still for there were yet no whales to be seen.

One night, those of us who had just been relieved from our watch on deck, were sitting on our sea lockers down below listening to stories about monstrous whales. It was dead calm, and one of those profoundly dark nights in which the very stars seem to be quite distant and faint. Right in the middle of a story about a giant man-eating whale by the name of "Black Death," I stopped the storyteller and asked a question.

"Tell me truly, mate, can a whale really sink ships and eat men alive?"

"My young shipmate," began the man, "whales can do almost anything. They can rise up like a mountain and crash down like thunder. They can stay at the bottom of the ocean for over an hour, then rise and swim faster than a bark. One little flick of its tail can turn several long boats into splinters, and wives into widows. Many a man has found a watery grave by forgetting what whales can do. Yes, laddie, whales can do monstrous things, and if you don't think they can swallow a man then you best remember old Jonah."

As soon as this sailor concluded his remarks, I noted that a few of the men that were listening, including Timothy Dronner, were beginning to look rather frightened. In an effort to conceal their fear, these men quickly and quietly made their way up the ladder that led to the main deck.

A smile slowly began to form on my face, as I viewed the actions of the not-so-brave shipmates who were unable to cope with a scary story. With the departure of these men, the storyteller apparently determined that he had accomplished his chief end, and soon grew silent and began to ready himself for a good night's sleep. After what seemed like only a few minutes, however, those of us who remained below deck suddenly heard a loud noise above us coming from the main deck.

A mixture of curiosity and fear caused several of us to immediately scamper up the ladder that led to the main deck, in order to discover the reason behind all of the commotion. Through the blackness and shadows, I followed the others to the point where we could see four men locked in mortal combat thrashing around near the stern. With great difficulty, I was able to recognize at least one of the men that was engaged in the donnybrook, and that was none other than Tim Dronner himself.

"No living man will call me a coward," shouted Tim, just before he took another swing at the man who had been part of the night watch.

The smiles on the faces of those of us who were watching this battle soon disappeared, however, as we saw Captain Flynn abruptly appear holding a lantern in his hand.

"Stand fast and stop your fighting," yelled the captain in an angry tone. He then added, "Gather near the mizzenmast straight off and explain yourselves."

Moments later, these men tried, each in his own way, to convince the captain of their innocence.

The agitated skipper was in no mood, however, to accept the feeble excuses that were offered by these men for their conduct. "You all know very well the rules I have set against this type of thing," began the captain. "Yet, you have decided to use the freedom and liberty that I have afforded you to violate the peace and security of my ship. You men have given me cause to regret my leniency."

"Begging your pardon, Captain," remarked my friend Tim, "but the men on watch called me a coward for failing to abide the scary stories that were taking place below deck."

"Hang your blasted pride," bellowed the skipper. "Your actions not only disrupted the sleep of several of your shipmates, but also endangered the entire crew, by taking men away from their vital duty as watchmen. You will be punished this night with ten stripes, you and the others who dared to place your pride above my clear commands. Mr. Owens, tie the offenders to the mast and administer the punishments I have set forth without delay."

"Very well, sir," replied the first mate.

So, in the company of the entire crew, the punishments were promptly administered under the dim light that shone from three small lanterns. Although some of the men involved chose at a later date to grumble and complain about the captain's approach to discipline, it clearly achieved the desired effect on the crew, for fighting among the men was rare indeed during the remainder of our voyage.

At the dawning of the following day, I decided to arise and help my friend Tim deal with the effects of the thrashing that he received during the night hours. Between the punches he had taken, and the stripes he endured from the whip, he was quite a sight to behold. Slowly and patiently, I administered a medicated salve to my friend's back and shoulders. Just as I was beginning to think that my efforts were going well, however, I heard Tim give out a short cry as if he were in pain.

"Did I hurt you, friend?" I asked.

"No, no," came the reply. "It was just that I thought that you might soon do so," he added.

"Well, now, aren't you the brave one," I replied, with a shake of my head.

Moments later, in an effort to change the subject, my courageous patient looked toward the sky and said, "Now this is going to be a grand soft day, indeed!"

As soon as my friend's remarks had left his lips, however, I heard the first mate, who happened to be walking by at that moment say: "Now, I wouldn't be too sure of that mate. I just checked the glass, and I think we may well have trouble brewing just ahead."

"Trouble, sir, on a beautiful calm day such as this?" I said.

"You are a green one for sure Mr. Surrey," stated Mr. Owens. "Seamen quickly learn that they can't trust their senses alone, or a white squall may sneak up on them with little or no warning and take them to the bottom. We look to the weather-glass or barometer to see what the pressures are, my boy. A high pressure front, for example, seldom means nasty business is coming our way. But when we see a low pressure front come up sudden like, then no matter what, we are in for trouble."

As I sat motionless, trying to take in all that the first mate had just told me, Captain Flynn came toward us and shouted for Mr. Owens to come to him. "A weather report, if you please, Mr. Owens," requested the skipper.

"I just checked the glass, Captain, and we are in a low pressure front, that's for sure. I don't think this fair weather will hold for long, sir. What are your orders?"

Under Sail at Last

"Have the men seal all the main hatches, and just to be on the safe side, get a crew aloft to shorten sail with all possible speed, Mr. Owens. A squall may well be headed our way, and I for one intend that we be ready to meet it if it comes calling."

As I ran to my post following the captain's orders, I still had trouble believing that we were about to confront a violent storm. After just a few minutes, however, I began to appreciate the skipper's judgement, for the winds and sea soon exhibited a dark and angry tone.

"Clew up those topsails, men," cried the second mate. "Make speed, men, rouse yourselves and take in every inch of canvas."

A loud roar could now be heard, as gale force winds soon began to rip apart the few remaining sails that had yet to be taken in. Thanks be to God that few men were left in the rigging at this stage of the storm, for the ship began to be tossed about until the yards were very nearly touching the water.

"It has all the makings of a white squall, Captain," shouted the first mate, as white foam and giant waves began to cover the main deck. "It is a good thing that you had us batten down the hatches, or we never would have survived that initial blow!"

"I'll wait till later to congratulate myself, Mr. Owen," yelled the skipper as he urged all hands to hold on for dear life. "Remain at your station, men, and I will do my level best to direct the helmsman so he can keep our ship from breaking up or capsizing."

As the captain endeavored to make it over to the helm, he soon found that the only way he could make any progress was on his hands and knees. As a result, the captain determined to swallow his pride, and began to crawl over towards the helmsman in the midst of the quickening gale. Upon arriving at his desired destination, Captain Flynn stood up and helped to steady the wheel.

"I don't think I can hold her much longer, sir," shouted the helmsman. "The winds are contrary, and I can't lay to in order to steady the ship into the wind!"

"If we can't swim against the tide, Mr. Billings, then we have little choice but to run with the wind in the hopes that we do not get swamped in the process," cried Argus Flynn. "Turn us about, now, and let us scud under bare poles!"

For over twenty-four hours, the storm continued to howl, while the sky and sea were as dark as the ace of spades. Those of us who waited below deck all this time, scarcely thought that we would live to see another day. Much to our amazement, however, the *Landsman* survived the horrific storm with little more than superficial damage. The skill of the man who steered our bark to safety was evident to all, and after the sun finally managed to peek through the cloudy sky, Captain Flynn made a point of thanking seaman Billings for his fortitude at the helm.

CHAPTER 6
There She Blows!

It took several days to complete the necessary repairs to our ship before we were able to resume our hunt for whales. The storm we had just survived had indeed damaged the *Landsman*, yet most of us were amazed that any vessel made by human hands could have withstood the fury of such a gale, and still remained relatively sound.

The chief carpenter on board our bark seldom had trouble keeping busy with one project or another. In the days following the storm, however, he suddenly found himself burdened with the extra task of directing teams of men to effect repairs to those portions of the ship that were damaged. By the time our vessel was put back in prime condition, I discovered that I had learned a thing or two about working with wood, as I was pressed into service more than once as a carpenter's apprentice.

As our newly refurbished bark sailed closer to Cape Horn, the captain set extra men on watch to ensure that we would not fail to spot any whales that crossed our path. Our skipper also ordered the first mate to inspect the long boats, to confirm that they would be ready to lower away at the first sight of our prey. Mr. Owens, therefore, personally inspected each of the four long boats that hung from the davits to ensure that they were properly outfitted. He began by examining the coiled rope that sat in each of the tubs, to see if the lines were neatly stowed and firmly connected to the harpoons. The first mate also examined the condition and positioning of the various lances, tools, and other equipment that were kept on board these vessels as well.

During this time of waiting and watching, my shipmate, the doctor, was attending to one of his first patients. This man had apparently managed to knock his head into one of the masts during the confusion and tempest of the proceeding week, and needed a fresh bandage placed on his head. Dr. Dronner was seated on the windlass, finishing up his first aid duty, while I sat near him sharpening a blubber-knife and practicing a new chantey.

As the minutes continued to drag on, I turned slowly toward my friend Tim and muttered, "When on earth do you suppose we will actually see a living, breathing whale? If all of these fancy stories about monster whales are true, why can't we spot at least one in these waters?"

"I guess like many a whaleman before us, Jim," replied my friend, "we are going to have to just wait and hope a bit longer."

At this point in time, it was evident that a great sense of anticipation was in the air, as well as in the hearts of many of my shipmates. As we sat waiting for some call to action. I could not help but wonder at this stage, what it would be like to actually spot my first whale at sea. As it turned out, I did not have to wait long to find out, for a sailor who was watching from the "crow's nest"—the place at the top of the masthead where a tiny platform is situated—suddenly cried out, 'There she blows!'

For the first time that season, the signal that a whale was in sight was heard. Not surprisingly, every man on board the *Landsman* was thrown into a state of tremendous excitement.

"There she blows!" roared the lookout again.

"Where away?" shouted Captain Flynn.

"About a mile off the port bow, sir," came the response.

The entire crew sprang to life as they gathered the tools of their trade in anticipation of the captain's orders. At the same time, the first mate ordered the sails to be taken in or shortened. As the ship began to slow down and settle deeper in the water, I ran over to the port side railing and glanced out to sea. Before long, a dark gray object looking something like a large floating log came into view. As I sought to get a clearer look at what I assumed to be a whale, I saw a dark gray creature rise up above the waves and shoot a thick stream of frothy water out of the top of his head some thirty feet in the air.

There She Blows!

While I stood leaning against the rail, lost in the wonder of this grand scene, the forty foot long creature suddenly slapped his giant tail or flukes against the blue-green sea, and disappeared into the deep. My excitement was such at this moment, that I seriously contemplated jumping in after the beast in order to prevent him from getting away. Thanks be to God, however, that I quickly came to my senses, and to the end of my courage for that matter, and abandoned this plan.

"To your stations, men, and stand by to lower your boats!" yelled the skipper.

"Very well, Captain," replied the men, as they moved into their appointed stations. Every man on board a whaler, right down to the cook, had his assigned post. For this reason, when Captain Flynn gave his command, sailors could be seen running in every direction, in order to get to their duty station.

"Now's the time to hunt, boys," shouted Argus Flynn with more than a little passion. "Lower away!" he commanded.

Within two minutes, three long boats were floating on the water, each with a crew of six men. The captain himself commanded one vessel as the headsman, and the other two boats were directed by the first and second mates. In spite of myself, I somehow managed to make it to my post in one of the longboats before it was lowered into the sea.

As soon as the lines were cast off, we were given the order to seize our oars and pull in the direction that the headsman signaled. No sooner had we begun to row, however, than a final shout could be heard from the crow's nest.

"I sight at least three fish dead ahead, sir," cried the watchman. "Big whales, maybe a hundred barrels each, as near as I can figure," he added.

After we moved away from the side of the *Landsman*, those of us in the boats saw two whales breach and then spout, not more than two hundred yards off of our starboard side. Before our headsman had a chance to speak, however, a third creature came into view. It was then that Mr. Owens could be heard shouting from one of the boats nearby; "It's a good day for whaling, lads, for we have found ourselves a whole school of whales. Put your backs into them oars, men, pull hard and earn your salt! "

In less than five minutes, we arrived at the spot where our headsman had directed us to row. By this time, however, none of our intended victims were in plain sight.

"Lay to on those oars, lads, hold hard now while we wait for them," spoke the captain, as he steered the boat in which I was stationed. "They won't be under for long; steady now boys, steady," he repeated in a softer tone of voice.

While our crew rested and caught its breath for several moments, we noticed that the first and second mates had decided to steer their boats in the direction of some whales that they viewed in the distance. Our boat sat alone, therefore, patiently waiting for our prey to come to the surface once again.

After a very short time span, the captain was pleased to inform us of the arrival of our large guest, for he shouted; "Look sharp, the fish are soon to rise!"

As if on cue, a giant gray beast came once again to the surface and swam close to where we had been waiting. We immediately began to row toward it with all of our might, as our captain began to urge us forward. His words were of little consequence, however, for we were all so primed for battle that we truly needed no headsman to tell us what we needed to do. As I rowed with all of my strength, I could feel my heart beating like thunder within my heaving chest. I began to wonder if the veins in my neck would be able to withstand the extraordinary pressure, but I had little time to dwell on this subject given the urgency of the moment.

As we were about to overtake our first whale, the captain spoke out from the stern saying, "Harpooner. Stand ready. Stand by your iron!"

The harpooner positioned himself in the bow of the boat, and balanced himself on a small platform that was mounted there. In a matter of moments, he reached over and grabbed a long iron shaft with a barbed point by its wooden handle. This weapon was attached to a long rope, which was coiled away in a metal tub that stood in the stern of the boat.

When the time was right, and we had rowed to within a short distance of the gray giant, our leader cried, "Give it to him, now. Strike him!"

Without the slightest hesitation, the harpooner raised the long shaft up toward the heavens and sent it deep into the side of his adversary. Almost immediately, the great fish lurched violently in response to the blow, an act that was not fully anticipated by our skipper.

"Hold fast lads," bellowed the headsman, as he saw that his tiny boat was poised to run aground on the whale's back.

"Give slack to the lines, and pull hard astern," added the captain in a desperate manner.

Well might the captain have been concerned, for as we floundered on the back of our prey for what seemed like several minutes, it became clear that our lives would all be lost if the whale flicked his mighty tail or flukes but once. By the mercy of heaven, however, the heaving giant determined to swim ahead, thereby providing us with the opportunity to back away to a safe distance. Just as we began slipping off the back of our intended victim, however, Captain Flynn managed to give him a deep wound with his lance.

"She is going to run for it, lads," shouted the captain. "Keep a sharp eye on the logger-head, and prepare for a rocky ride!"

The moment the captain finished his remarks, we all held our breath as we watched the wounded beast throw his huge tail high into the air in order to strike the sea with a loud thunder. This act nearly capsized our long boat, and sent a shower of foamy white salt water directly in our faces.

Before we could fully recover from this insult, the great mammal began to distance himself from our tiny vessel. "Hold the line, or we will lose this fish for certain," screamed our headsman at the top of his lungs.

It may help to explain at this point, that the line that was connected from the harpoon to the boat we were sitting in, traveled around a large wooden post that sat in the stern called a 'logger-head.' This post enabled us to control, at least to some degree, the amount of tension that we felt was proper to keep at any given moment on the line that held us to our fish. In cases where a whale determined to run fast after being struck, it would often require one of the crew to pour water over the logger-head, in order to keep the heat that was caused by the friction on the rope from causing a fire. As one may well imagine, it took a great deal of skill and courage to work the line during a battle with an angry whale. One wrong move could well mean disaster, for too much tension on the line could burn it up or, worse yet, drag the entire crew below the waves.

Holding on for dear life, my shipmates and I watched as the linesman did his vital work. As our rope strained to keep pace with the animal we were pursuing, I began to fear that one of our men might get his leg or arm caught in the line that jerked so wildly in our midst. Every moment that went by as we sailed across the surface of the water, I fully expected that we would be pulled under the waves. Just at the point when our doom seemed certain, however, a bit more line would be let out and our future prospects would improve dramatically. In those cases when a long boat did get pulled under the waves, the men described this as "a stove boat."

After an extended period of time, the mighty creature finally began to grow tired of dragging us across the water at top speed. As we hastened to take up the slack in our line, and coil the excess back in its proper tub, our skipper began to plot how best to finish off our foe.

"Pull forward, lads, and bring me alongside of this fish before she gathers her strength once again," commanded Argus Flynn. "I have a mind to finish her with my lance!"

Our brave captain never got a chance to act upon his plan, however, for the whale we had pursued for such a long time suddenly decided to lower his mighty head and dive for the bottom. As soon as he began to "sound", or throw himself under the waves, we felt our boat jerk back slightly and settle peacefully on the blue-green waters.

In a matter of moments, we discovered the reason behind this strange development, for the harpooner cried, "Our line is free, and with it our fish!"

The harpoon that had held us fast to our prize for so long apparently decided to give way. As we all sat in silence, not knowing whether to laugh or cry, I well remember the awful feeling of disappointment that flooded my soul. As it turned out, however, none of us had the chance to stew in our juices for long, for a shout was soon heard in our ears. The cry came from one of the men in the other longboats.

"Ahoy, shipmates, come and help us if you can!" cried the first mate in a tone that revealed his desperate condition.

We all turned at once, and saw that the first mate and his men were indeed in a tight spot. Our mates had managed to get a line into a large sperm whale, and were flying across the

surface of the sea at a speed that can only be described as dangerous. A clear indication that they were enduring a treacherous "Nantucket sleigh-ride" was soon confirmed, as we noted that they were flying a distress flag from the top of an upright oar.

"Well men, it's up with the sail, for our fish is gone and our shipmates need help with their catch," said the captain, as he struggled to forget the whale he had just lost.

A fresh breeze began to develop, as three of the men in my whaleboat labored to set and unfurl the sail that was positioned in the center of our thirty-foot long vessel. Once the sail was in working order, we quickly cut across the water and came to within fifty yards of our distressed companions.

"Let out more line, Mr. Owens," shouted our leader, as the boat we were pursuing flew across our bow at an alarming rate of speed.

"Nothing doing, sir," replied the first mate. "We are at the end of our line, and must hold hard or perish!"

"I don't like the look of things, Captain," said one of my shipmates who stood near the rudder.

"Nor do I," responded our skipper, "but we will follow them at a distance notwithstanding, and hope for the best."

The words of our captain had barely been uttered, however, before we all witnessed a scene so terrible that it literally took our breath away. As you might well guess, the calamity we beheld involved none other than the crew that was under the command of Mr. Owens. In full view of us all, the line that connected the first mates craft to his prize whale suddenly snapped, thereby causing his boat to tip wildly and capsize.

For a brief period we could see no sign of life, or of a long boat for that matter, and we began to despair. Sailing on, however, we soon discovered to our great relief that Mr. Owens and his crew had managed to survive, and were now clinging precariously to their overturned whaleboat. Moments later, we arrived at the spot where the survivors were located, in order to see how we might be of assistance.

"Are your men accounted for, Mr. Owens," asked Captain Flynn.

"We are all accounted for sir," replied the soggy first mate. "I believe, however, that two of my crew are banged up pretty good. We could sure use a hand righting this boat of ours, Captain."

With great difficulty, and more than a few scraped knuckles, we managed to right Mr. Owen's whaleboat over a period of several minutes. After this was accomplished, we then helped our mates to locate several of the oars and other items that had been cast overboard during their mishap. As soon as our rescue efforts were completed, a number of the men in our group began to feel rather sorry for themselves, as they considered how little they had accomplished for all of their labors.

As the captain endeavored to bring a word of cheer to his downcast shipmates, he was interrupted by the sound of men yelling in the distance. A large grin soon appeared on the face of Argus Flynn, as he watched his second mate go gliding by him stuck fast to the very whale that he had previously lost. In the midst of trying to deal with all of his troubles, as well as that of his first mate, Captain Flynn had quite forgotten that he still had one more whaleboat in active service.

"Well, Mr. Owens," said the skipper plainly, "it appears as though our fortunes may yet improve this day. Is your boat fit for further service, or should we sail on without you?"

"You best sail on to help the second mate, sir," came the reply. "My ship and my men are both spent, so, with your permission we will make our way back to the ship."

"Permission granted, Mr. Owens," remarked the skipper. "Have the crew on the *Landsman* stand ready, should we capture our first whale," he added.

In less than a minute, Argus Flynn had our whaleboat turned about and headed in a leeward direction. Since we fully expected to be in the thick of the hunt in a matter of moments, the skipper ordered us to drop sail, and to row in the direction of the sperm whale that we had previously engaged. At the urging of our leader, we somehow summoned the energy to dig our oars into the sea and narrow the distance that lay between ourselves, and the sperm whale we were seeking.

As we approached the scene of action, we could see that the second mates crew was busy taking in some of the line that had slackened while their adversary had begun to tire and slow his pace. Without any hesitation, Captain Flynn ordered us to advance towards the side of the lumbering giant, in order

There She Blows! 49

to strike him with yet another harpoon. We soon made our approach, therefore, in much the same way we did previously, but this time the harpooner sent his weapon squarely between the third and fourth ribs of the creature and straight into his vitals.

    Immediately after the harpooner had finished his work, our leader commanded us to pull away from the thrashing whale so that we might avoid the fury of his flukes. As we sat at a safe distance, our crew watched the mortally wounded giant go into his final "flurry" and then roll over on his side. A brief period of silence soon followed, as both crews sat in the midst of a crimson sea admiring their first catch of the season.

"Well done, men" shouted the captain, as he shook the hand of the harpooner who was responsible for delivering the fatal blow. "Now, let us fin out and set the tow-line fore and aft to secure our prize, lads."

So, when our work of securing the sperm whale to our boats was accomplished, we rowed slowly back to the *Landsman* amidst a steady stream of cheers and song. While my work as a whale hunter was nearly over for that day, my job as a chanteyman had just begun. I sang out, therefore, a lively song known as 'Heave Away, Johnny', as my shipmates and I towed our hard-fought treasure over to our little wooden home.

Chapter 7
A Floating Butcher Shop

I am pleased to tell you that Mr. Owens and his crew were able to make it back to the *Landsman*, while only being a little worse for the wear. Two of his men had broken bones, one a leg and the other an arm, yet the rest of the crew was still fit for duty. Our gratitude for the safe arrival of Mr. Owens aboard ship soon became even more intense, however, when we realized that one of his first acts as the senior officer was to maneuver the *Landsman* in the direction of where we were awkwardly towing our sperm whale.

Those of us that were involved with the process of towing our first whale, were greatly relieved to finally make it back to the safety of our ship. This experience clearly taught men like myself how difficult it was to tow a massive and slippery whale across an uncooperative ocean, even when the sea was relatively calm. During our brief but arduous journey, we utilized both sail and oar to propel our long boats in the proper direction.

Upon reaching the starboard side of our whaling bark, two men equipped with long ropes and chains took the first critical step of tying off both ends of our prize. One of the men was lowered down to the narrow or "small" section at the base of the flukes in order to attach a chain around it, while the other man did the same around the creature's lower jaw.

Once the men had secured the sperm whale to the *Landsman*, I began to entertain the foolish notion that our work was nearly done, and that our crew would soon be able to enjoy a long period of rest. Nothing, of course, could have been further from the truth, for it was soon apparent that after a short break we would need to begin the process of "cutting-in" or butchering our catch. Since whaling barks like ours never stopped in ports to obtain help in cutting off the blubber from their whales, or in extracting the precious oil that they supplied; all of this work had to be done by sailors such as us.

Captain Flynn did permit those of us who had lately returned from hunting whales to change into some dry clothes, and to catch up on our rations, before beginning our next assignment. While we were relaxing for a few minutes, and enjoying a sumptuous meal of stale beans and hard tack, some of our shipmates began the task of setting up a large wooden platform called a "cutting stage." This structure was positioned along the side of our ship in such a way that it would reach out over the carcass of the whale, and rest not far above the surface of the water. The cutting stage provided a stable place for the men to work from as they endeavored to remove the blubber from the carcass of the whale they were butchering.

As soon as my meal was finished, I decided to take the few minutes that remained in my break to study the fascinating creature that was now bobbing next to our tall ship. While I walked toward the sperm whale that was chained securely to our vessel, I noticed that several of my mates were in the process of setting up a huge winch, with heavy block and tackle, between the main mast and the foremast. I assumed correctly that this equipment would soon be used to help lift the heavy pieces of blubber from our cutting stage to a large storage room on board our ship.

I eventually made it over to the starboard side rail, and began to peep over the side in order to get a better look at the whale we caught before it was butchered. After a short period of time, the second mate noticed that I was studying the features of the gray giant with a rather puzzled look on my face. He must have felt that I could use a lesson on whales, for he walked over in my direction and began to speak.

"Well, Mr. Surrey," he began, "you look a mite confused. Since you are green, and quite new to this whaling business, let me give you a lesson or two on the species of mammal that hangs below us just now."

After the second mate adjusted his cap slightly, he continued by saying: "The body of this sperm whale is nearly fifty feet in length, and twenty feet around at its thickest part. Its

A Floating Butcher Shop

head alone is over fifteen feet long, and as you can see, has a very square and blunt appearance. If you look for a nose on this beast you will not find one, for sperm whales have a single blowhole in the top of their head that takes the place of a nose. This species of mammal, known as a cachalot, does have ears but they are hard to see for they are only about the size of a walnut and sit right behind the enormous eyes that are on each side of its blunt head. The lower jaw of the sperm, which is somewhat shorter that the upper portion, contains a rather long row of large teeth that weigh a pound and a half each. These teeth, together with the substantial jawbone that is prominent on this type of whale, are prized by those sailors and ship builders who like to fashion them into works of art. The most precious oil in a cachalot, resides in its enormous head or "case," and for many years this was utilized to anoint kings and for other special purposes.'

"The sperm, like all whales of its kind, is covered with a thick layer of blubber, which helps to keep them warm as they swim in the cold ocean depths. Their blubber can get as thick as twelve inches wide, especially if they frequent arctic waters, and has the added benefit of helping them to regulate the pressure that works on them so powerfully as they dive or "sound" quickly to the bottom.'

"As you can see, Jim, the sperm whale has flippers on each side of its body which act to steady the giant as it swims swiftly under the ocean waves. These flippers work much like the limbs of land animals, and are fed by a supply of blood vessels and nerves. The real work of propelling this mammal through the sea, however, is done by its mighty tail. The sperm below us just now, has flukes that span a distance of fourteen feet, but I have seen other whales like it that were much wider. As you might guess, Jim, the tail has other purposes beside motion. When threatened, the sperm whale uses his powerful flukes as a weapon, and at times when he is at play, the gentle giant enjoys slapping his tail against the surface of the water. What's more, this creature uses its tail when he throws himself out of the water in order to peak and dive.'

"The sperm whale or cachalot loves to swim far and wide, and has been spotted swimming in all of the oceans of the world at one point or another. This mighty mammal can hold its breath for up to an hour, and swim to depths that would crush a man. When under the ocean waves, creatures such as these like to eat squid, cuttlefish, or small sea urchins. On rare occasions, however, sperm whales have been known to feed upon sharks or porpoises.'

The two species of whale that are the most sought after by whaling men, are the sperm and "right" whales. Although we have yet to see a right whale in these waters, it is only a question of time before we cross paths with one of these giants. Unlike the sperm whale, the right has a very large round head and huge mouth that has no teeth. In place of teeth, it has the well-known substance called whalebone, or baleen, which grows from the roof of its mouth in a number of broad, thin plates. These plates extend from the back of the head to the snout. The lower edges of these plates of whalebone are split into thousands of hair-like bristles, so that the inside roof of the right whale's mouth resembles an enormous brush! These bristles enable this strange creature to catch the little shrimps and small creel on which it feeds. When it desires a meal, therefore, it simply opens its large mouth and rushes into the midst of a school of tiny sea creatures. As soon as the whale has obtained a large enough mouthful of its prey, it shuts its lower jaw and swallows what its net has caught.'

"Well, much more could be said about such giants of the sea, my young shipmate," said the second mate, before adding, "but the captain has work he needs for us to do just now."

As soon as the remarks of the second mate ended, I heard Mr. Owens call me to the main deck in order to join a work detail that was in the process of being formed. After I was issued the necessary gear and equipment, I was eventually stationed with a group of men who were responsible for hoisting the large strips of blubber called "blanket pieces" on board the *Landsman*. Before long, men stationed just below us on the cutting platform began cutting the blubber off of our first whale, and then we heard them yell, "Hoist away!"

The men that I labored with quickly taught me how to lower the large iron hook, known as the blubber-hook, to the cutting men so that they could attach it to the top of the strip of blub-

A Floating Butcher Shop

ber they were working on. After the hook and lines were in place, we then proceeded to pull down with all of our strength in order to lift the massive strips of blubber high enough to be deposited in our blubber room. Our task as heavers, for that is what we were called, was hard in the extreme for we had to hoist numerous blanket pieces weighing at least one ton each high over our heads, aided by only the ropes and pulleys. More often than not, the first pieces to be hoisted on board were relatively light. I was told some time later, that it was thought wise to start with the hauling of smaller pieces such as the fins, just to ensure that the block and tackle equipment was in good working order. It was, of course, vital that our system of winches and pulleys were operating properly, for if they gave way, several men could be crushed to death beneath the tremendous weight of the blubber sheets.

The job of cutting the whale into manageable chunks, was usually done by five men. Four sailors stood on the cutting stage and hacked at the carcass of the whale with long-handled spades or digging knives. The fifth man, armed as he was with a sharp blubber knife, spent most of his time positioned on the body of the whale, wherever he was needed most. To prevent tragedy, this cutter had a life-line tied about his waist at all times, just in case he fell off of the slippery mammal into the sea.

These five men began their efforts by separating the head of the sperm whale from the main body. The long blunt head of the sperm was then sectioned into three parts. The top half of the head or "case" contained the purest oil, and this was commonly retrieved with the use of a wooden bucket. The lower portion of the forehead or "junk" yielded both spermaceti and oil. Spermaceti was a fatty substance that was often used in the making of ointments or candles. The final part of the head contained the upper jaw, along with the lower jaw that held the teeth and tongue.

The tongue, which was as large as a cow, was of little practical use other than for food. Whenever we captured a whale, therefore, it was likely that we would soon be staring down at bits of whale tongue in our ration of stew or soup. The teeth and jaw bones, as I have already mentioned, were greatly prized for scrimshaw, or for use by those who were trimming out whaling ships such as ours.

Once we had hauled the various components of the head on board, the rest of the flensing or cutting-in was a bit less complicated. Continuing at the neck area, the cutters simply sliced large strips of blubber off of the animal in a spiral fashion, not unlike the peeling of an orange, until they finally reached the tail.

The huge blanket pieces that came off of the whale's body were slowly dropped, one-by-one, into the blubber room where three men were stationed. These workers were responsible for cutting the massive blankets of blubber into smaller so-called "horse" pieces as soon as they arrived at their station. Once this additional cutting was done, the men could more readily move and store the blubber in their hold. Even after the blubber was cut into horse pieces, however, it was still rather difficult to handle, for the pieces were nearly a foot thick and very slippery. Little by little, notwithstanding the difficulties involved, the blubber room on the *Landsman* slowly began to be filled with the precious oil-rich remains of our sperm whale, much to the delight of Argus Flynn.

While our crew was busy processing its first whale, I noticed the arrival of a growing number of sea birds. I was soon informed of the fact that such birds always keep company with whalers, so that they might feed upon the scraps of food that are regularly available during the butchering process.

As I finished talking with another shipmate about this subject, a mature albatross floated skillfully toward us on the wings of the wind. This was perhaps the largest bird I had ever seen, and little wonder, for no bird that flies has a wider wingspan. Soon after that, another sea bird arrived; and, although we were hundreds of miles from any shore, this did not keep us from being surrounded by flocks of gulls, giant petrels, cape skimmers, and other sea faring birds. These creatures lost no time in beginning to feed upon the pieces of the whale's carcass that were now exposed, in an effort to pick it clean. After a brief period of feasting, these greedy birds could only fly away with great difficulty.

On one occasion, late in the afternoon, a close friend of mine managed to capture a rather large albatross as it landed for several moments on the railing that surrounded the quarterdeck. Much to the amusement of all on board, this mate strutted around the main deck and forecastle showing off the features of his new feathered friend to whoever had enough courage to venture close to it. I clearly remember petting the soft white feathers of this majestic creature, and marveling at his strange webbed feet. If my memory serves me, I believe that this bird had a wingspan that measured nearly ten feet.

Unfortunately, birds were not the only animals that our crew had to contend with during the cutting-in process. One group of unwelcome animal guests that were particularly troublesome to the cutting men who worked directly on or near the body of our whale, were sharks. Many of these beasts were over ten feet long, and were armed with three rows of razor

A Floating Butcher Shop

sharp teeth. As the men worked to strip the whale's carcass, these villains would hurl themselves into the side of our lifeless prize in order to gain a meal, and in the process, to steal as much of our profits as possible.

As I stood at my heaving station just above where the cutting men worked, I often observed very clearly how close the sharks would come to the men who were stationed near the surface of the water. When we first began our work, I would cry out, "Shark, Shark!" nearly every time I thought that one of these man-eaters was getting too close to one of the sailors. I soon discovered, however, that I was the only one bothering to yell out a warning to those who were in harm's way. Finally, I determined to ask the second mate: "Why am I the only one making an effort to sound the alarm, sir? Doesn't anyone but me care about the safety of the cutters?"

"We care, sure enough, Mr. Surrey," replied the second mate calmly. "But the danger posed by these sharks is already well known to the men working below, and your shouts will likely only serve to alarm the cutters and put them in greater danger. We know that you mean well, lad, but you might as well save your breath on this account."

"I think I understand, sir," I remarked, while shrugging my aching shoulders.

"Besides," added the officer, "if a shark gets too close for comfort, the men on the cutting platform will use their long-handled spades to help fend off the trouble makers. On more than one occasion, I have seen a shark receive a mortal wound from the end of a sharp cutting knife, and drop into the sea. When this happens, then the other sharks quickly turn against their wounded companion and feed upon him greedily. Most sharks, therefore, are content to wait until we cut our fish free before feeding on its remains."

Although I still had my doubts, I was obliged to honor the words of the second mate, for he was far more experienced in matters concerning the habits and dangers of sharks. Several days later, I also learned that whaling men like to hunt sharks, for they use the rough skin of this beast to make a type of sandpaper that is useful for polishing and cleaning.

Shortly after the incident with the sharks, our crew cut the last piece of blubber off of our cachalot. After this achievement, Captain Flynn inspected the inside cavity of the whale, searching for a treasure known as ambergris. This special substance, worth hundreds of dollars a pound, was used to make expensive perfume. Few whaling men ever found ambergris, however, for it was normally only found within the body cavity of a sick whale.

After the inspection, the order was given to cast off the useless remains of the whale. Once the carcass was unfastened, it sank slowly under the ocean waves, much to the displeasure of the birds which had yet to feed upon it to their satisfaction. But what was loss to the sea birds was gain to the sharks, for these savages were well able to follow what little was left of our sperm whale to the bottom and pick it clean.

Even when the sharks and whale were gone, however, there was still plenty of danger to contend with on board the *Landsman*. The oily juices that seeped out of our whale during the initial cutting-in stage, made it difficult for sailors to walk about without falling down or slashing themselves on knives or sharp equipment. Apart from the slippery conditions, crewmen were also at risk as they began to dismantle the cutting-stage, as well as the other heavy equipment that was part of our elaborate winch and pulley system. Nevertheless, there was still a certain degree of relief that took place in the minds of both captain and crew after a whale was finally butchered and his carcass released.

For this reason, we all breathed a little easier when the first officer cried, "The cutting-in is done, men. Now let us ready and stoke up the fires in our try-works; look sharp, ye whale men!"

"Hurrah, Hurrah!" responded the crew in unison, as every sailor began to prepare himself for his next assignment.

Now that we were largely done with the business of butchering our first whale, we could move on to the work of extracting or "trying-out" the oil that it offered us.

Chapter 8
Oil and Trouble

The life of a whaleman on the high seas is very unpredictable, and often bounces between great extremes. One minute he is floating on a calm sea trying to find something to occupy his mind, and the next minute he is in a life and death battle with a whale, or perhaps a violent storm. If you gave most whaling men the choice, however, they would much rather face the difficult or even dangerous circumstances that sometimes confront them at sea, rather than have to deal with the long periods of intense boredom.

When sailors on a whaling bark have little or nothing to do, the days seem to stagnate into dreary nights. Under these circumstances, the men find it hard not to dwell on the painful fact that they are separated from family and friends. In fact, I once remember asking Captain Flynn if he ever missed his loved ones back home in New Bedford town. He was, as I recall, a bit taken back by my inquiry and stated:

"Of course, Mr. Surrey, why do you ask?"

"Well, begging your pardon sir, but you are not known to speak of them often," I explained.

"It is true that I seldom speak of them before the men for, in my experience, such remarks only tend to breed a sense of gloom or melancholy amongst the crew. I will, however, confess to you privately that I miss my dear wife and children more than words can say. My wife and children are my gold and sunshine, and it pains me to speak of them at any length. I write home as often as I can, but since the *Landsman* seldom puts into port, my ability to get messages back to New Bedford is rather limited. My best hope, and that of other home-sick sailors on board our fair bark, is to cross paths with another ship that is homeward bound, and willing to deliver letters on our behalf."

"Do you think that all the grief associated with such long voyages is worth it, Captain?" I asked, as I contemplated my own heartache.

"Well," began the skipper as he sighed, "if a man wishes to gain a living from the sea by catching whales, then he must go to where the fish run. I have never yet met a whaling man who caught a single whale from his parlor or seaside mansion."

When the simple but profound words of Argus Flynn came to a close, my only response was to slowly nod my head in order to acknowledge my agreement with his sentiments.

I share these thoughts with you now, at this point in our story, in order that you might be able to understand why whaling men seldom complained when they were faced with the dirty and smelly business of trying-out the oil from a whale. Although such labors were not exactly pleasant, the men on board barks such as ours still preferred them to the alternative of inactivity. Whatever else may be said about the difficult and dangerous job of extracting oil from a whale, at least it kept the men's energies and minds well occupied.

The day after we finished cutting-in our sperm whale, the captain called our entire crew to the main deck at seven bells. As soon as we were assembled, our leader spoke saying, "We have a fine day with calm seas, men. It will be a good day to finish the trying-out of our first whale. However, before you set to work this day, lads, you will first join me aft to splice the main brace!"

For the benefit of those who have never been whaling, I will explain that Captain Flynn was calling the men to join him for a brief celebration featuring strong drink. This act was one of many time-honored traditions on whaling barks from the earliest days of sail, and was designed to keep the morale of the men high as they went about completing difficult and demanding chores.

It was not long, therefore, before the captain could be seen handing out the traditional jug of grog to the men who had gathered around him. Although I passed over the grog, I did appreciate the fact that our skipper also decided to have a truly decent meal dished out to us that morning, complete with hot

Oil and Trouble

rolls and dumplings. This festive celebration was welcome, indeed, but it was not long before Mr. Owens was calling us to resume our labors.

Our crew was soon divided into two watches, each taking a shift of six hours of hard labor in the morning, and then again in the afternoon or evening. Our first order of business, was to set up the "try works" where we would eventually boil out the oil that we needed to extract or purify. The try works consisted of two, or sometimes three, huge iron melting pots

that were mounted upon brick fireplaces that sat between the fore and main masts. The base of each fireplace had a thick layer of sand and stone in place, in order to keep the heat and sparks from the fires from damaging the wooden deck that sat below them.

The first mate ordered four men to build a fire under each of the try pots, so that our work could begin in earnest. The fire at each trying station was initially started with small wooden logs, but as the hours passed, these fires were eventually fed with the oily scraps of blubber that were readily available to us.

As soon as the first mate was satisfied that the try works were safe and ready for service, he ordered some of the men to boil out the choice oil that came from the whale's head or case in order to ensure its purity. Most of the other men from our work crew were sent down to the blubber-room, to help cut up the remaining blanket pieces into the smaller horse pieces. Hour after hour, men were assigned the task of standing near tall and sturdy blocks of wood, called "horses," so that they might slice the smaller chunks of blubber with mincing knives into uniform slices known as "Bible leaves." The chunks of blubber were slashed in an effort to help them melt more easily, and in this condition, they resembled the pages of a book.

On a regular basis, the men at the try-pots would shout, "Bible leaves! Bible leaves!" to indicate that more of the processed chunks of blubber needed to be thrown into the melting pots by one of the sailors. As the boiling oil rose in the pots, it was bailed into copper cooling tanks. Eventually, this oil was then transferred into standard wooden barrels, and stowed away in the hold of our ship.

As nighttime approached on the *Landsman*, the fires from the try-pots began to glow redder and brighter, and to cast a strange light upon our bloody deck. It was by this light, as well as by the glow from some well-placed lanterns, that we continued with our dirty and slippery work well into the evening hours. At one point that evening, as I began yet another shift of work, I suddenly thought to myself, 'The shopkeeper in New Bedford town sure knew what he was talking about when he said that whaling was wet and dirty work!'

Oil and Trouble

Just when I was getting rather sick of looking at another basket of blubber, the time finally came for our work crew to retire for six hours of welcome rest. As I slept, the new watch kept the fires burning, and continued to try-out the blubber from our recently deceased cachalot. When I awoke, I walked over to the windlass, and sat down to enjoy yet another delicious meal consisting of beans and stale biscuits. While I began eating, a shipmate by the name of Connel Pence sat down beside me. Connel was, like myself, among the younger members of the crew, and we seemed to get along well from the start. This particular morning, however, my friend seemed uncharacteristically agitated as he pointed to his arm and said in a sluggish manner:

"Greetings, shipmate. I hope you are having a grand morning, because mine is considerably less gleeful."

"What's the matter, Connel?" I asked, with a voice that reflected my concern.

"Oh, I managed to burn my arm during the last shift on that blasted try works station, that is all," he replied. "It hurts like blazes, and I can't hardly sleep."

"Have you paid a visit to Tim Dronner for some first aid treatment?" I inquired.

"I thought about doing so, Jim, but I'm not so sure he can help," replied the injured man.

"I can't help if you don't let me try, shipmate," remarked seaman Dronner as he happened to walk by and overhear our exchange.

"I meant no offense, mate," explained the young sailor, as he held out his damaged arm, "but I know your skills are limited."

"Rest easy, mate, for I take no offense," replied Tim Dronner. "Yet, hear me when I tell you that I think that I may have just the right cure for what ails you. Step over here and sit with me, while I clean your wound and apply some aloe vera ointment to speed your healing."

"Very well, Tim, lead on and I will follow," said the mildly embarrassed sailor.

Five minutes later, the discouraged burn victim named Connel was in much better spirits. He stood up from the bench he was resting on while receiving his treatment, and remarked: "Well, Dr. Dronner, the ointment you applied has soothed my wound and provided me with considerable relief. I am grateful for your efforts, and will be sure to put in a good word with the captain on your behalf."

"See that you do, shipmate," concluded seaman Dronner, "for I can use all the help I can get to stay in the captain's good graces."

As the two men parted ways, I could feel a sharp wind begin to buffet our sails and rock the ship slightly. Looking over in the direction of Mr. Owens, who was strolling slowly in my direction, I remarked, "I fear we are going to have a breeze, sir. If that is the case, we may yet have more burn victims."

"A storm at this hour would be unwelcome for many reasons, Mr. Surrey," stated the first mate, as he walked over to my side. "First off, it would force us to put out our fires in the try-works, and that is difficult business in rough seas. Many a sailor has been scalded in times past, as he worked to put down the fires. My greater fear by far, however, is if we fail to trim our fires in time, the winds may end up carrying fire to other parts of the ship. Just last year, the schooner *J. Truman* caught fire in this very way, and sank to the bottom with all hands."

I never found out how the fire got out of control on this schooner, for at that moment the captain came on deck, and gave orders to furl the top gallant sails. Three or four of my shipmates were soon climbing upward on the rigging with a right good will, and in a few minutes, the sails were lashed to the yards.

The wind soon began to blow steadily from the nor' east, but not with enough authority to stop our try-works for any length of time. A hour or two later, however, the wind picked up again and caused the seas to swell to such an extent that we were compelled to slack the fires. Much to the delight of Captain Flynn, this minor tempest was short lived, and never did develop into a dangerous gale. For this reason, it was not long before our fires were, once again, burning brightly under our try-pots.

While our work resumed, Argus Flynn and Mr. Owens walked together near the quarterdeck, and began to speak with one another during this period of relative calm. I heard the captain say: "I think, even now, we may well be carrying on too much canvas aloft, Mr. Owens. Send men to the rigging, so that they may take in the reefs in the topsails. We are in no hurry to leave these waters, what's more, we still have to finish trying out our oil. The more trim and stable we can make our craft at this stage, therefore, the better."

A few minutes later, just as it was beginning to get dark, I heard the first mate yell out an order from the quarterdeck to shorten sail and clew up the topsail yards. Upon hearing this command, the men who were already perched in the rigging began to re-position themselves in order to complete their next assignment. Although it was growing darker by the minute, I could still see two of my shipmates, Shawn Hammer and Samuel Kottle by name, climbing up the shrouds in order to

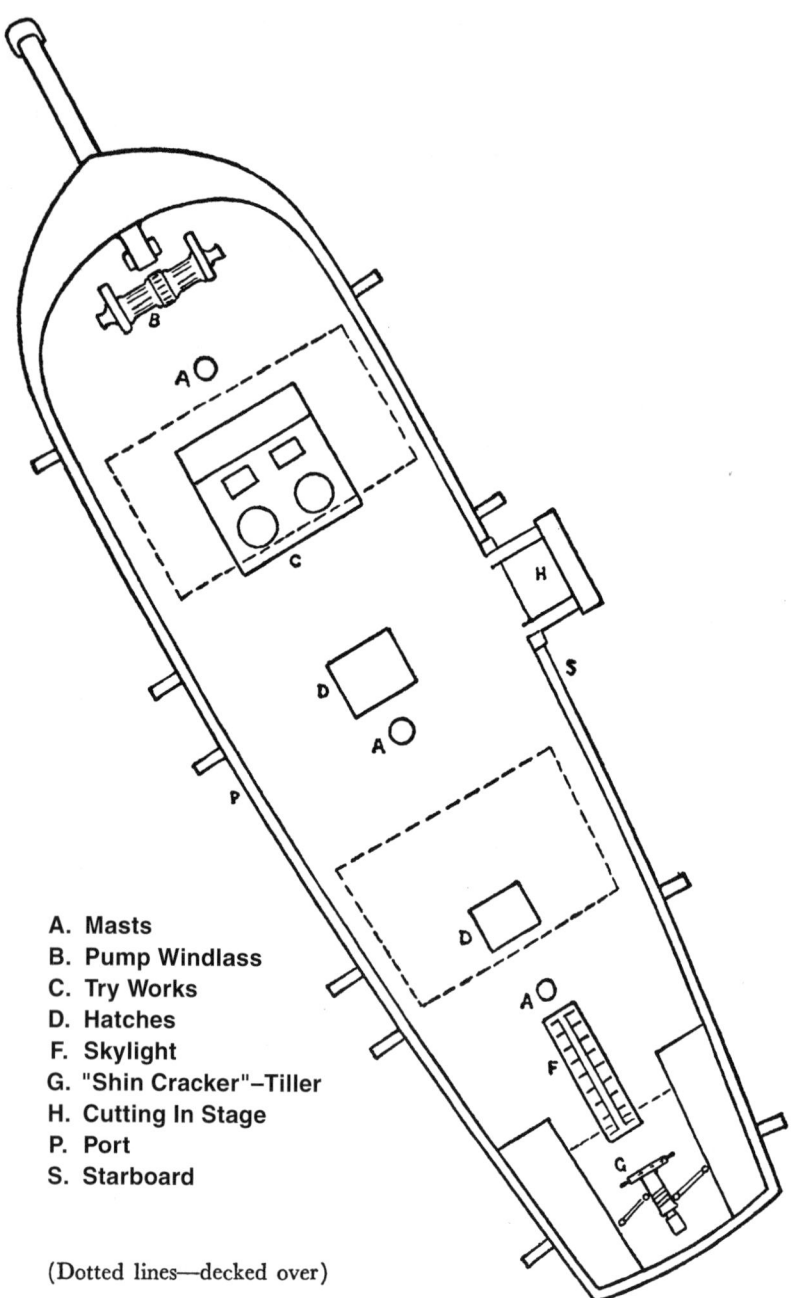

A. Masts
B. Pump Windlass
C. Try Works
D. Hatches
F. Skylight
G. "Shin Cracker"–Tiller
H. Cutting In Stage
P. Port
S. Starboard

(Dotted lines—decked over)

Deck layout of typical whaling vessel

lay out on the topsail yards. Just as I was about to look down, I thought that I saw a large object fall from the far side of the yards. Moments later, my worst fears were realized, as I heard a faint scream, followed by a pronouncement from the lookout stationed far above. He cried, "Turn about. Man overboard!"

I must confess, after hearing this dreadful news, I very nearly froze in my tracks with fear. As quick as a flash, it dawned on me that the sailor who had just tumbled into the sea may well be my close friend, Shawn Hammer. While I struggled to regain my wits, thankfully, men like Argus Flynn were not in the least bit shaken by the ordeal. In what seemed like the span of but a few heartbeats, I heard our skipper shout:

"Prepare to turn about with all speed. Clew up the mainsails, men, and stand by to lower away at my command."

"Very well, sir," cried the first mate, as he began to bark out his own orders to several of the men.

While the crew sprang into action, I saw the second mate throw not one, but two, water barrels into the sea from the stern quarter of the *Landsman*. Standing as I was near the tryworks station, his actions inspired me to thrust a small bundle of oil soaked logs into the nearby fire, and then, just as quickly, to fling them over the side. In no time at all, I could see the blazing logs shining faintly on the surface of the water as they quickly moved astern of our position at a startling speed.

Notwithstanding the best efforts of Argus Flynn, our ship was hard pressed to turn about in the direction of our fallen comrade. Our ship's head had already been thrown into the wind, in an effort to come about with all possible speed, but great care needed to be taken by the captain, for our fires were still blazing in the try-works.

As I stood looking out to sea in the direction of Shawn Hammer, for I learned that it was indeed he that had fallen, I could barely see any sign of my burning logs. It was at that moment, that I began to lose hope, and think that perhaps none of us would ever see him again in the land of the living. As despair began to grip my soul, I suddenly recalled the words of advice that I received from Rev. Carlson, "Cast all your care upon the Lord, Jim, for with God nothing shall be impossible."

Right then and there, I determined to call upon the Lord, in spite of the fact that everything within me seemed to say that all was lost. Although I had permitted the worldly atmosphere of a whaling vessel to compromise my prayer life and Christian testimony, I did earnestly pray, then and there, that my messmate might be saved. I cannot say that my prayer, generated as it was out of desperation, was very impressive to God; still, the simple act of crying out to the Almighty afforded me some genuine comfort. It is often at times such as these that the Lord chooses to remind us of how helpless we really are as creatures, and how utterly dependent we are on him for life, safety, and success.

After what seemed like an eternity, the captain was finally in the position to order his men to ready themselves in the long boats. Once things were in order, he shouted, "Lower away the rescue boats!"

I was relieved to hear the words of the skipper, and made sure that I was placed in the first boat that was to be lowered. As soon as we reached the water, I began to pull on the oars with all of my might.

The second mate, who was the headsman of our boat, held a lantern out to his side with one hand, while he guided the rudder with the other. By its faint light we could see but a short distance off, for the moon shone only a sliver that night and the darkness was very great.

"Do you think that we have any chance of finding him, sir?" I asked.

A shake of his head was his only reply, until a strange noise was heard in the distance.

"Pipe down, men," said the second mate, "for I thought that I heard some one cry out."

We all stopped our chatter, and tried to identify the true source of the sound, between the noise of the whistling wind and waves.

"I think that I see something, sir," said one of the sailors, as he pointed to a spot off the starboard bow.

"For pity sake, man, tell me where," shouted the man who was holding the rudder.

"Two points off the starboard bow. Look, now do you see it?" he asked.

Before the officer could respond, however, our boat shot past a small water barrel that was floating on the ocean waves, with the figure of a man clinging stubbornly to it.

"Hold hard! Stern all!" yelled the officer, as we endeavored to come around as quickly as possible.

In our zeal, we had managed to row right past our shipmate, and I instantly became concerned that we would lose him again in the blackness. The fear of losing Shawn caused me to panic, and I let go of my oar and prepared to jump into the sea to effect his rescue. Thanks be to God, however, that Ben Lodins had the presence of mind to seize me by my arm just short of too late, in order to prevent me from leaving the boat. Several moments later, after I received a stern tongue lashing from the second mate for attempting to jump ship, we reached the water barrel and rescued Shawn Hammer.

He was nearly done in by the cold and by general exhaustion, but he still looked mighty good to those of us who had fished him out of the ocean. It did not take long to row back to the *Landsman*, and by the time that we arrived back on board, our soggy shipmate was already beginning to recover strength and vitality.

Shawn lost no time in giving glory to God for his rescue, but also made a point of thanking those shipmates who risked their lives to save his own. In particular, however, he was also quick to express gratitude for the man who had the presence of mind to toss the flaming timbers in his direction.

"I never would have seen that floating barrel, if it weren't for that precious beacon of light," added Shawn, through shivering lips.

"I don't rightly recall who it was that released those burning timbers," remarked the second mate, as he adjusted his cap.

"Nor am I in any position to say so," added another member of the crew. "Perhaps it was an angel!"

"Don't you worry about that question now, shipmate," insisted the second mate. "You are safe and sound, and that is all that matters."

Within a few minutes, we were all enjoying a hot mug of apple cider, and talking about most anything other than our recent ordeal. The rescued sailor, meanwhile, was given a fresh set of dry clothes, and a heavy wool blanket for good measure. A warm lantern was also placed near his feet, so that he might recover quickly from his chill.

As several of the men from our crew stood staring at Shawn Hammer, who by this time was starting to read a passage from his Bible by the dim light of the lantern, the captain walked up and bellowed: "All right ye blooming bunch of nannies, stop your staring now. In case you hadn't noticed, we still have work to do on this here bark. Mr. Owens, order the fire stoked and the men to resume their duties. The wind has slackened, once again, and we must finish with our fish by morning so we can sail out of these waters."

"Aye, aye, Captain Flynn," came the reply.

CHAPTER 9
Searching for Water

When the last of the whale oil was stored safely in the hold, we set sail in a southeasterly direction for the whaling grounds just off the cape of South Africa. By this point in our voyage, however, Captain Flynn began to recognize that our supply of fresh water was beginning to run low. For this reason, he determined to seek out a place where we could replenish our stores of the precious liquid.

Several of my shipmates were suffering from severe stomach aches, and at least one had a nasty case of dysentery. These men, therefore, were particularly glad to learn that the captain was determined to obtain clean drinking water as soon as possible. Since our ship was not close to a suitable port, it was likely that we would need to locate a large island along our route in order to secure the water we needed. Under normal conditions, we were able to replenish our supply of fresh water by simply catching rain in large barrels that sat on our main deck. For several weeks, however, almost no rain had descended upon us from the heavens, so our need for water was becoming more urgent with each passing day.

One morning during this crisis, I was awakened by the first mate Mr. Owens. He shouted at me to make speed and join the crew on deck in order to hear Captain Flynn. He then added, in a rather grumpy tone, "If you know what is good for you then you will not delay, for the captain is in a foul mood this day."

As I stumbled up the stairs that led to the main deck, I noted that the captain was standing next to Mr. Owen with a long thin wooden rod in his hand. It did not take long for our skipper to state the reason for calling all hands on deck. He began, "Well lads, it would appear that we have a thief on board our fair bark. You all know well the order that I gave a fortnight ago that placed all hands on half the standard ration of water. Now, the first mate reports to me that our water stores have continued to go down beyond measure in spite of my command. Be it known to all, therefore, that any man who is caught taking more than his allotment of drinking water will be cast overboard or marooned on the first available island. This wooden world of ours has no room for thieves, and I fully intend that anyone among us that will not mend his ways shall die without mercy. Go back to your stations men, and pray to the weather gods to send us rain, or at least an uncharted island that can yield us water."

Three more days past, and still the thirsty crew of the *Landsman* had yet to catch sight of land in any form, nor as much as a single cloud in the sky. As it happened that very night, a sailor named Samuel Kottle was caught trying to break into the water barrel that stood near the forecastle. He had been standing duty in the night watch, when he determined to defy the captains orders. He was immediately clapped in irons, and taken to Captain Flynn's quarters.

"Send him to the brig this night," ordered the skipper. "I will deal with this brigand at eight bells."

True to his word, Captain Flynn had the prisoner brought before him on the main deck for trial early in the morning. With the entire crew assembled, our leader proceeded to ask the accused sailor a few direct questions. Seaman Kottle made no pretence of his innocence, but simply sought to petition the captain for leniency.

"Since you seek to claim no innocence in this matter," began the captain, "I will proceed with your sentencing. I hereby order that you be bound hand and foot, and tossed into the sea. Mr. Owen, see to it that my orders are carried out to the letter and promptly," added Captain Flynn.

"Very well, sir," replied the first mate, just before he heard a voice from the crow's nest cry aloud; "Land ho, land I say!"

Every eye was soon fixed upon the horizon, as the skipper walked over to the starboard side of the *Landsman* in order to use his looking glass.

"Where away?" asked the captain to the lookout who was perched high above him.

"An island, sir, due west," came the quick reply.

In a matter of moments, Captain Flynn was scanning the horizon with his looking glass, and then calmly remarked: "An island it is, a right big island. Strange, but I do not recall seeing this body of land on my charts, but there it is nevertheless."

"What are your orders, Captain?" asked Mr. Owens.

"Prepare a landing party to go ashore with all speed," replied the skipper. "With any luck, we will find some fresh water at this spot, and perhaps some provisions as well."

"Very well, Captain. May I also assume that you intend for us to maroon seaman Kottle at this island as well?" added the first mate.

"I will think on the matter of Kottle, while you labor to ready the landing party," responded the captain.

In less than an hour, a crew of eight souls, including Mr. Owens, Shawn Hammer, Tim Dronner, Samuel Kottle, and myself were slowly rowing a johnnyboat toward the island. Our flat-bottomed craft was filled with a number of empty barrels and water kegs, as well as with several large canvas bags that were suitable for carrying fruits or vegetables.

Before we reached the shore, Samuel Kottle made a point of thanking Mr. Owens for helping to spare him from being tossed overboard.

"I may have helped to save you from a quick death at sea, lad," remarked the first mate, "but you may yet live long enough on this desolate island to wish that I had never taken up your cause."

"If the skipper would have given me leave," replied the condemned man, "I would have explained that I took the water to try to rid myself of dysentery."

"Your reasons may be clear to you, and perhaps you deserve better, but there is no denying the fact that your actions endangered the lives of every one of your shipmates," said Mr. Owens. "With some good fortune at your side, you may yet

Searching for Water

survive on this island. Who knows, perhaps another ship may rescue you from this prison before it is too late."

A thick silence fell upon those of us who were rowing the boat toward shore, as we contemplated the exchange between the first mate and the sailor named Kottle. For my part, I could not help but commit Samuel's case, no matter how flawed with human error, to the Lord.

As soon as we were about to ground our small vessel upon the sandy shore of the remote island, the first mate ordered us to ship our oars. Moments later, four of my companions sprung from the bow of our boat in order to pull it forward and secure it safely on the beach. Mr. Owens, who was the leader of the landing party, then directed us to make our way inland with several of the water kegs and barrels.

"Captain Flynn has ordered us ashore to gather fresh water, firewood, and provisions with all possible speed," bellowed the leader. "We will begin our mission without delay, therefore, and head up in the direction of those hills in the distance," added the first mate as he pointed the way. "If we are to find suitable water on this island, it will likely be in the hill country. Forward, men!"

It took several minutes for our tiny band to move across the sandy beach, and around a series of large boulders that stood in our way. This task was made all the more difficult, as a result of the fact that we were obliged to push several heavy barrels in front of us as we marched. Eventually, however, our procession reached an area of flat ground that was covered with scrub grass and an occasional palm tree. Once we began to move across this firmer ground, we made much swifter progress toward our objective.

As the sun began to slowly move up higher in the sky, we finally reached a group of gently sloping hills that stood before a series of cliffs. At this point, Shawn Hammer was the first person in our party to identify a small waterfall situated in the cliffs that were now coming into view.

"Should we make for the falls, sir?" inquired Shawn.

"Yes, by all means, seaman Hammer," replied the leader of the expedition. "The day is moving fast, and we must fill these kegs and get them stored in our boat before nightfall."

Before long, tired and sore, we arrived at the falls and were grateful to find them quite suitable to our purpose. A small pool or spring sat just below the falls, which greatly aided us in the process of filling up our kegs and barrels. Best of all, as soon as we arrived, the first mate gave us the liberty to drink freely from this spring before finishing our task, an act that greatly refreshed us all.

After we had finished filling our water kegs, we all sat down for a brief period of needed rest. After several minutes, however, my friend Timothy Dronner summoned the energy to climb a large palm tree that sat nearby in order to secure a few coconuts. It was not long before I heard a call in the distance, and saw my friend walking towards me with a long knife in one hand, and two coconuts in the other.

"Jim, Jim Surrey, come and help your old shipmate," yelled my friend. "I have played the part of the monkey, and have gathered more coconuts than I can carry," added Tim with a chuckle.

"Go help your friend the monkey," commanded Mr. Owens as he shook his head slowly. "We have need to be gone from this place without further delay."

With two canvas bags full of coconuts, and several barrels and kegs of fresh water, the eight of us began our slow march toward the beach. The afternoon was now nearly spent, and I could tell by the look on the first mate's face, that he was getting anxious to return to the boat.

"Speed lads," ordered Mr. Owens, "we need to get the water and provisions stored and make our way back to the ship while the winds are still favorable."

"What about the firewood, sir?" questioned Shawn Hammer. "Captain's orders, you know."

"Now you just let me worry about that detail when the time comes," replied the leader. "With any luck, we will be able to secure an ample supply of driftwood near the beach that will suit our purposes."

On and on we pushed our tired bodies, as we labored to reach our destination before the sun began to sink. Finally, much to the relief of the first mate, we reached the boat and stored our goods on board just before sundown.

"Well men, before we shove off and leave this island and its newest occupant," began Mr. Owens, "it is still needful for us to comb the beach in order to secure firewood. Get to it shipmates, spread out and do your work quickly. Oh, seaman Kottle, I think that it is best if you stay near me at this stage."

With little zeal, and even less daylight, our party began its hectic search for firewood along the beach and near the rocks that sat nearby. After just a few minutes, we all heard a shout coming from the direction of Samuel Kottle and our first mate. Turning round, I was able to see the man who was destined to be marooned, push Mr. Owens in a rather violent manner. I then heard a scream coming from the lips of the young seaman, as he began to cut at the ground with a sword he had in his hand.

Rushing over, I helped to pick up the leader of our party, and then noted that Kottle was now sitting on both knees and evidently in a great deal of pain.

"What on earth has happened here, sir?" I asked.

"That man, Samuel Kottle, has just saved my life at the expense of his own," cried the first mate with great emotion. "There, among the rocks, see for yourself!"

Taking several steps to my right in the direction of my fallen comrade, I saw the remains of a rather large black viper, and no small amount of blood.

"That's right, shipmate," said Mr. Owens, as I continued to stare in his direction, unable to speak. "A pit viper was poised to strike me, when the man I was going to maroon grabbed my cutlass, pushed me to safety, and took the blow."

Just after these remarks, I heard a low groaning sound come from the direction of the valiant victim. With the help of Mr. Owens, and one other sailor, we managed to help our stricken mate up from his knees, for he was already nearly too weak to stand.

"Thank you friend," said the seamen in a soft voice, "but I'm afraid it is only a matter of time. The beast struck me full on, and that can only mean one thing. Oh well, perhaps it is for the best. I wasn't looking forward to living alone on this island anyway. You best get back to your ship men, for there is nothing that you can do for me now. Pray that the Almighty might look kindly on my poor soul, the soul of a thief and brigand."

"Men," said the first mate with firm determination, "this noble man is right. We can do nothing more for him here. But I am determined, with your help, to bring him back to the ship in order that he might be given a burial with full honors before the eyes of all his shipmates. That is the least that I can do for the man who has saved my life. Come then, let us leave this sad place without delay."

And so it was that with heaviness of heart, and no shortage of tears, that we rowed back to the *Landsman*. As it turned out, our friend and shipmate Samuel Kottle never made it back to the ship alive. In spite of our best efforts to comfort and aid him, he soon began to breath very strangely, and then gave up the ghost.

I am happy to say, however, that Mr. Owens was true to his word, and spoke up boldly for his benefactor. For this reason, after the first mate had finished delivering his full report to the captain, Samuel Kottle was indeed tossed overboard into the sea; but in a manner quite different than originally planned, for it was with full honors and the esteem of all his shipmates.

CHAPTER 10
Big Jack, the Fighting Bull

It was not easy for myself, or the other men, to put the sad end of Samuel Kottle out of our minds. Nevertheless, we eventually were forced to do so, in order that our ship could function properly. Weeks passed as we slowly made our way to the Crozettes' hunting grounds just off the tip of South Africa, picking up an occasional right whale or overzealous shark along the way. We had already been at sea for several months at this stage, and yet, our only stops had been for fresh water at remote islands on our outward-bound track.

Much to the delight of Captain Argus Flynn, who lately seemed to be in an agitated state of mind, we reached the South Sea whaling grounds off Cape Town. The captain had made a point of steering our whaler into seas that were well known for harboring giant sperm whales, some as long as seventy feet. He was tired of catching "suckers" or "calves" as he called them, and pledged a gold coin to the first man who sighted a big "school-master," or bull sperm whale.

One day, I turned to the first mate, Mr. Owens, and asked, "What's been eating the captain?"

After several seconds of contemplation, the tall and seasoned officer simply shrugged his shoulders and said, "He wants to catch the biggest sperm whale in this here sea. If you must know, I reckon he's after Big Jack himself."

"If ye don't mind me asking, sir," I continued, "who is this creature named Big Jack?"

"Why only the fiercest bull in all the four oceans, my young shipmate. He is marked by virtue of the five lances that protrude from his lumpy back, like so many peacock feathers. It was last fall that he was spotted in these waters, and I only hope that if we meet up with him that we fare better than the last hunting party."

"Why would that be, Mr. Owens?" I asked.

"The last time whaling men went after this monster, he managed to stove three boats and kill nearly a dozen men. The legend of Jack grows each year; some say that he has sunk whalers and killed over a hundred men. Others believe that he is a ghost, and can't be captured or killed."

"Ye are not trying to frighten me with one of those wild stories about monster whales are you, sir?"

"I say what I say," asserted the first mate, sharply, as he slowly walked away.

Moments later, as I approached a group of shipmates who had just finished their watch, one of them shouted, "Chanteyman, give us a song!" "How about *Carlingford*?" added another mate.

As the men gathered around me, amidst the swaying of the sails, I lifted my voice and sang the opening verse:

"When I was young and in my prime and could wander wild and free, there was always the longing in my mind to follow the call of the sea."

The assembled shipmates then provided the chorus to this old favorite by singing:

"So I'll sing farewell to Carlingford, and farewell to Greenore, and I'll think of you most day and night, until I return once more, until I return once more."

I then continued, "On all of the stormy seven seas, I have sailed before the mast, and on every voyage I ever made, I swore it would be my last."

After another chorus, I ended by singing, "Now, the landsman's life is all his own, he can go or he can stay; but when the sea gets in your blood, when she calls you must obey. So I'll sing farewell to Carlingford and farewell to Greenore, and I'll think of you most day and night, until I return once more, until I return once more."

As the noise of the song quickly floated away from the assembly, an even more delightful voice could be heard in the distance crying, "Supper, laddies!" The thoughts of the men soon turned to their stomachs as they prepared to feast on bread, soup, and a special ration of plum pudding.

A predictable hush fell over the men as they began to concentrate on their eating. I sat down next to my friend, Ben Lodins, who was talking with the second mate about the difference between the right whale and the sperm whale.

Although I had already learned about some of the differences between these great whales weeks before, I still listened intently as the second mate stated, "Sperm whales are known to swim in all of the world's oceans, however, most species of right whale seldom venture into the warmer South Seas. Both creatures can grow to an enormous size, particularly in the case of the males or "bulls," but they look quite different from each other. The right whale has a very round head that contains two large blowholes, while the sperm has a relatively thin, blunt head with one small blowhole. A seasoned lookout can easily tell the difference between these two whales, simply because the sperm has a fairly weak spout that is very close to the front of his head, while the right whale spouts from the middle of his head with much greater force."

"The female or cow sperm whale is commonly only one-third the size of the male or bull cachalot. The female right whale, on the other hand, is considerably larger than the female sperm, and generally prefers to breed in shallow waters."

Ben Lodins, who was quite well acquainted with whales in his own right, went on to describe the habits and might of the sperm whale by adding:

"The sperm whale not only feeds in a different manner than the right whale, it fights differently as well. The mature sperm whale is more aggressive than the right whale, which often tries to flee after it has been struck. Sperm whales are noted for their aggressiveness after being wounded, and will sometimes turn on their foes and smash their boat with a blow of its blunt head or tail. Wise old sperm whales, called 'bulls,' which have become clever through experience, give sailors the greatest trouble."

"On occasion, particularly during breeding season, sperm whales are not only in the mood to attack men and long boats, they even attack each other! I well remember seeing, during my first voyage out, two big bull sperms go after one another. When their big blunt heads collided, it sounded like the clap of thunder. The sound could be heard nearly a mile away. The two combatants then withdrew from each other to rest, but this truce did not last long, for they soon were at it again trying to break each other's jaws. After these two giants finished mauling one another, they were so tired and bruised that we had no difficulty whatsoever capturing them a short time later."

"Although it is not common, sperm whales have even been known to sink whole ships. Perhaps the most well known case involved the whaler *Essex*, and demonstrates the risk sailors take when they go after fighting bulls. Permit me to recount this amazing, true story."

"In the year of our Lord, 1819, the American bark *Essex* sailed from Nantucket bound for whaling grounds off the west coast of South America. This craft was under the command of Captain George Pollard, Jr. Late in December of the same year, the *Essex* rounded Cape Horn, and received some extensive damage during a squall that it encountered. Rather than turn back, Captain Pollard pushed on to the whaling grounds he was seeking, arriving in October of 1820. When in latitude 40 degrees of the South Seas, the crew of the *Essex* finally came across a 'school' of sperm whales. Three boats were immediately lowered and sent in pursuit of the sperm whale pod. The first mate's boat was struck by one of the bulls during a chase, and it became necessary for this vessel to return to the *Essex* for repairs."

"Shortly after the crewmen arrived back to their ship, they began to try to secure the damaged boat to the davits. As soon as this was accomplished, an enormous whale suddenly rose quite close to the ship. He was going at nearly the same speed as the *Essex*, about three knots. The men on board the ship could easily see that this giant sperm whale was no less than eighty-five feet in length. All of a sudden the monster started to act very strangely, and then rammed its head into the side the ship, causing considerable damage to the hull. The whale immediately dove and passed slowly under the ship, causing it to tip from side-to-side. This act apparently injured the giant bull, for he suddenly rose to the surface about five hundred yards off and proceeded to lash the sea with his tail as if in great agony."

"Before the men on the *Essex* could even begin to effect repairs on their ship, however, it began to fill and settle lower in the water. It was then that the beast seemed to recover its strength, and swam straight at the bow of the stricken ship at a frightful speed. While the sailors worked frantically at the pumps in order to try to save their ship, one of them shouted:

"'God have mercy! He comes again!'

"Sadly, this report was all too accurate. The whale had indeed turned, and was rushing headlong at the wounded ship with a great fury. The creature then smashed into the weather bow, driving the 283-ton vessel backwards, crushing it in. Moments later, the mighty sperm whale dove into the deep and disappeared."

"The frightened sailors took to their long boats at once, and in a matter of minutes, the *Essex* sank down beneath the waves. Much has been written about the long and terrible journey that these survivors endured in three open boats far out upon the sea, with little in the way of provisions."

"Tell me, Ben," I asked. "How many men survived?"

"Out of a crew of twenty men, only eight survived to tell their amazing story. After several miserable weeks at sea, most of the men died of starvation, dehydration, or exposure. The sailors that managed to live through the ordeal, were forced to feed upon the remains of their fallen shipmates, and endure a thousand hardships."

As my shipmate Ben Lodins prepared to continue his talk, a loud cry could be heard coming from the crow's nest.

"There she blows! Big whales off the starboard bow!"

This unexpected alarm made us all spring to our feet in an awkward fashion. As the *Landsman* maneuvered into position for the hunt, the deck hands strained their necks to be the first one to sight a big bull whale. Every crew member longed to get the gold coin that was pledged by Argus Flynn.

"There she breaches! There she blows!" cried the lookout, once again.

The captain soon appeared on deck and shouted, "Where away?"

"Sperm whales, about two miles off the starboard beam, sir."

Without as much as a word from the captain, every man moved into his proper position or station. After nearly a year at sea, our crew had become so accustomed to the routine that we scarcely needed to be told where to station ourselves.

"Keep us informed of their position," barked Captain Flynn as he moved to the poop deck.

"Aye, aye, Captain."

"Keep her squarely into the wind," ordered the captain to the helmsman. "Mr. Owens, fetch me the looking-glass."

"Steady, keep her dead ahead," came the cry from the poop deck.

"Steady it is," replied the helmsman.

Captain Flynn, positioned as he was at the stern of the ship, suddenly pointed aft. Moments later we learned why the captain was trying to draw our attention, for we heard a loud clap behind us, followed by a heavy splash. Turning around, we saw the flukes of a giant sperm whale sweeping through the air not more than two hundred yards astern of our position.

"Come about, helmsman," shouted the captain. "Clew up the mainsail and lash the yards. All hands to your positions, and prepare to lower away."

"Prepare to lower away" repeated the second mate, with a voice that thundered. In a flash, all hands were on deck and ready for action.

"Ready the lowering lines at the davits," uttered the anxious captain as he joined one of the crews. "Lower the long boats."

In the twinkling of an eye, our boats were lowered into the sea. We pulled away from the *Landsman* just as the large cachalot breached for the second time, less than a mile away from our position.

I occupied my usual place in the captain's whaling boat, next to the loggerhead, and close to where Argus Flynn himself steered. Every man in the captain's boat was personally chosen by him, therefore, since we had no slackers, we soon left the other two boats behind us. Thanks to the instruction of Ben Lodins and the second mate, I had no trouble in identifying our target as a bull sperm whale. If fact, every one of my shipmates quickly agreed that this creature was likely the largest sperm that we had encountered since putting out to sea.

As we worked at the oars, and moved rapidly across the surface of the water, a small calf suddenly breached near us on the starboard side. The tiny creature must have been in a playful mood, for it immediately sent a shower of mist over our boat, and then slowly slid down into a pool of foam. Seconds later, another whale rose calmly on the opposite side of our boat, only to be joined by another small calf off our starboard bow. Much to our delight, we found ourselves in the middle of a school of whales, which proceeded to spout and gently roll around without any awareness of our violent intentions.

It was not long before the patience of our leader was rewarded, however, as the large bull whale that we noted prior to leaving the *Landsman* came once again to the surface. By the aggressive manner in which this giant breached, we knew that we were in for a challenging hunt. After blowing on the surface once or twice, about a half mile off, he raised his flukes and propelled himself under the waves.

"Our big fish has sounded, lads. Ship your oars and rest easy, for he will likely be down for a while," remarked Argus Flynn in a confident tone.

On this occasion, however, our leader was mistaken, for the prize whale had only gone down deep in order to gather enough momentum to spring out of the water with reckless abandon. While Argus Flynn and the rest of us gazed at this unexpected turn of events, several of my shipmates gave a shout of surprise and alarm. Little wonder why, for this huge whale had managed to leap clear out of the water not a hundred feet from our small whaling boat.

As we watched with our mouths open wide, the awkward creature came down on his side with a thundering crash. He then rolled his big white belly under the waves, and plunged his massive gray head beneath the sea. A mountain of spray burst from the spot where he landed, and just when we were getting ready to move, the creature disappeared beneath the waves once more.

"I still wonder, Captain, if that bull is not Big Jack," shouted the harpooner.

"Not likely," responded Captain Flynn, "but it is quite clear that he's a prize that is well worth pursuing. Pull, ye sheep heads. Spring to those oars, lads, for we must capture that whale whatever it should cost us."

As we began to pull away at the oars, I quickly noted that the other boats in our hunting party were not in any position to join us, for they were busy pursuing their own fish. This fact did not seem to trouble any of the other men, so I determined not to dwell on the fact that we would have to battle against a massive angry bull all by ourselves. At this point, the thrill of the hunt had clearly enabled all of us to suppress our fears, and to focus on the business of capturing a truly magnificent whale.

"There she rises," said our leader in a calm voice, as the brute rose up on our leeward side.

Big Jack, the Fighting Bull

Thanks in part to the skillful steering of our captain, we were able to maneuver our craft until we got to within a few yards of the monster who was riding slowly near the surface of the water. As we strained our backs in order to try to keep pace with the giant, he slowly turned to windward and spouted from his big square head. At this point, the captain suddenly ordered the harpooner to stand up. The anxious harpooner answered the call and raised his weapon, as he prepared to strike the blow.

"Strike him!" cried Argus Flynn, as he worked the rudder.

Moments later, the harpooner skillfully buried his long shaft deep in the side of our prey.

It was not long before we heard the command: "Stern all! Come about for your lives," as we sought to distance ourselves from the fury which we knew was soon to come. This maneuver was just in time, for, in his rage, the wounded whale jerked his tail up right where our vessel had just been. As we looked up to see where our adversary would decide to bring down his massive flukes, we were relieved to discover that he had determined to bring them down flat on the sea, with a loud clap that made our ears ring.

For a brief moment, I thought that we were going to be crushed to death, but we soon found ourselves out of immediate danger. Needless to say, we were soaked to the skin by the spray sent upon us by the frantic whale. All we could manage to do at this point, however, was to lie on our oars and watch the wounded monster sweep his great flukes against the surface of the water time and again. It was not long before huge mountains of suds began to form on the surface of the water, mingled with traces of the creature's blood.

After several more moments the sperm whale ceased his thrashing; yet, before we could row over and lance him, the clever mammal plunged deep into the sea. This unexpected maneuver took our line out quickly, but not so fast as to spin our boat completely around. In a manner not unlike a runaway freight train, however, the desperate whale began to pull us forward at a greater and greater speed.

"Hold on hard, and tuck in the stern sheets!" yelled our leader, as he struggled to remain calm. The next moment, we were flying across the sea at an alarming rate, while the waves threatened to swamp us. I instinctively began to pray to the Almighty, as our predicament became more and more life threatening. As I glanced around the boat, I was somewhat comforted to see that several other men were also conversing with their Maker and pleading for mercy. Never before had I experienced so much danger.

In the midst of our danger, we all heard some wild screams coming from off our starboard side. As we glanced over in the direction of this noise, we suddenly saw another whaling boat being pulled across the surface of the sea. It was the one that belonged to the second mate, and this vessel was also enjoying a rather hardy Nantucket sleigh ride in its own right. We then noticed that a pair of bottle nosed dolphins was coming up every now and then near our swiftly moving vessel, hoping perhaps that we had time to play with them.

As the anxious minutes passed, our line finally began to slacken, as the creature we had harpooned finally began to tire. At the command of our headsman, we hauled our line in hand over hand, and coiled it away in the tub that was located at the stern of the boat. During this momentary pause in the action, Captain Flynn took his place in the bow and prepared to utilize his lance. The whale soon surfaced and we promptly rowed toward him. This time, however, the clever giant did not run away, but turned around and headed straight for our little boat.

I was now so certain that destruction was at hand, that I did not even bother to panic. In my mind, it was only a question of time before we would feel the wrath of the huge gray sperm bull that was coming down on us like a battering ram. As it turned out, however, my assumption was in error, for our harpooner bravely reached out and savagely jabbed the head of the whale, causing him to turn away in a different direction to avoid the pain.

We continued to pursue the wise old bull, seeking for the right moment to finish him off. Just when our own strength seemed to be ready to give way, the angry whale changed direction slightly to one side, and Argus Flynn skillfully hurled the lance solidly into his vitals.

"That's touched his life," cried the harpooner, as blood flew up from the creature's blowhole. This was evidence that the mighty giant had been mortally wounded. We soon discovered much to our dismay, however, that our battle was far from over. With no little amount of awe and admiration, we watched the bleeding sperm begin to swim forward once again and felt the rush of the waves under our keel. Captain Flynn made every effort to get another lance in the side of our intended victim, but the bull would not cooperate. We then tried to hold fast, but the great mammal sounded too deeply, so we had to loosen our line to prevent our boat from being stoved.

As it happened, we apparently let out a bit too much line, for suddenly the rope began to get jumbled and to come out of its tub.

"Watch out, shipmates!" yelled the captain, as he tried to clear the line.

His efforts did not meet with success, however, for he soon slipped and fell. I then determined to come to the captain's aid, and reached over in order to protect him from the whirling line. Much to my surprise, before I could even react, a section of rope whipped around my right arm. I immediately felt a tremendous pressure on my arm as if it were about to come out of the socket, and in a moment I was pulled over the side. As I plunged into the sea, it soon became rather apparent that I still had my wits about me. For this reason, I was fully aware of my desperate condition, and began to cry out to my Maker even as the whale continued to pull me down farther into the depths. As a dreadful pressure began to build up in my ears, all I could think about was whether I would live to see another sunrise."

Before I could contemplate my circumstance further, I felt myself slowly rising toward the surface. Even to this day, I still have no idea exactly how I became freed from the rope. More than likely, however, it happened because the Lord caused the creature that was pulling me to slow his pace, and some slack developed in the line. As hope renewed itself within me, I began to buffet the water in an effort to reach the surface. Just when I was about to lose consciousness, my head finally broke the surface of the water.

After I came into the land of the living once again, and looked about me, I saw our whaling boat a mere sixty yards away. Even with an injured arm, I still felt confident that I could swim over to the boat, although I knew it would not be easy. A few moments later, my shipmates heard my cry, and began to row toward me. It then dawned on me that the sperm whale we were chasing must have ceased to run, for the men in the longboat were slowly rowing in my direction, although some were busy coiling rope. Before they had traveled more than fifteen yards, however, I watched in horror as the monstrous head of a whale shot up like a rocket out of the depths, not five feet away from my comrades.

I heard my shipmates scream, but they might as well have saved their breath, for even in my dazed condition I knew what was about to hit them. A terrible crashing sound soon pierced my ears, as I saw the mortally wounded monster fall with great authority upon the helpless sailors. As I braced myself to deal with the wall of water that came violently in my direction, I heard the pathetic cries and moans of the men mingled with the sound of cracking wood.

When the wounded giant had finally spent himself in his death flurry, he only had enough strength to slowly roll about and strike at the surface of the sea. Slowly but surely, I began to see pieces of the broken boat beginning to float upon the waves before me. What is more, and much to my surprise, I also started to see one after another of my shipmate's heads appear as the mist began to clear. In the midst of the blood and foam, these survivors soon began to swim toward any object that was floating in the water.

Providentially, the overzealous whale had overshot his target by a few feet; otherwise every man aboard would surely have perished. It was not long before I was able to join my comrades in the search for something upon which to float. My strength was nearly gone, before I managed to locate an oar that had come within my reach.

Just then I heard a cheer, and the next time I rose on the swell, I looked round and saw the first mate's boat headed for the scene of action. After what seemed like a long time, I was finally hauled out of the ocean by men from the third boat. By God's grace, no sailors were killed in the hunt; although one of them had a broken arm, and another a sprained ankle.

After the captain was fished out of the cold waters, he ordered the remaining boats to secure the wounded whale who was about ready to breathe his last.

"We won't let him get away, Captain" shouted the first mate as he grabbed his lance and ordered his men to attack. Two minutes later, Mr. Owens gave our valiant foe one last stab, and then retreated while the animal began to move into its death roll.

As I began to watch this terrible monster slowly die, I could not help but feel a sense of loss and regret for helping to destroy it. Even though we had engaged in a fair fight, it still felt as though the mighty Creator may have even been frowning a bit at the loss of one of His grandest living creatures. But the thought quickly left my mind, as the whale became more violent and finished his death flurry. We gazed silently at this scene, with hearts torn between remorse and jubilation.

Several moments later, the struggler ceased, and his carcass rolled over belly up in death. The calm that followed was quite amazing, after all the minutes spent in noisy battle. The silence, however, soon gave way to cheers; although even this act did not last long, for we were soon engaged in the urgent business of tying off our catch. The process of towing the sperm whale to the *Landsman* required the rest of the afternoon, for we had over four miles to cover before we could tie off our prize.

As our crowded boat came closer to the *Landsman*, the first mate began to stare into the distance with a strange expression of fear and wonder.

"Mr. Owens," I called. "Have ye seen a ghost, sir?"

Without any comment at all, the first mate simply pointed off the starboard bow to a huge gray creature with five lances protruding out of its back.

As the crusty old bull swam angrily by, no one could find the right words to speak. In this instance, words were quite unnecessary; for it was evident to all that we were staring at none other than Big Jack himself.

CHAPTER 11
Death on the High Seas

Under normal conditions, the whale that we had just taken would have been enough to gratify the sternest captain. It was clearly our largest catch to that point in our voyage, and produced over eighty barrels of fine oil. Nevertheless, Captain Flynn was still agitated about losing his chance to capture Big Jack. In fact, it might be more proper to state that our leader was fast becoming obsessed with bringing in this legendary bull.

Although sailors are as prone to grumbling about their lot as any group of fallen men, the plain truth was that our voyage had actually gone rather well up to that point in time. It goes without saying that not everything that we had endeavored to accomplish during our outward bound track had gone our way, for my story does not provide you with a full account of every event that happened during our whaling voyage. Still, when measured by the common standard of whales captured and oil gained, we were clearly ahead of our quota at this stage of our journey. Our prosperity was such, in fact, that some men were openly stating that we might be in a position to return to our home port in New Bedford before our time, if our success continued to hold.

By the evening of the second day after we spotted Big Jack, we were already finishing up the cutting and trying out of our tenth whale. Everyone, with the exception of the captain, was in good spirits and looking forward to a great season of hunting. One of our crew was particularly happy at this time, for he discovered a chunk of the valuable substance called ambergris as he helped to process one of our recent catches. During a lull in our work, I sat listening to the captain as he called all hands to the main deck.

"Mr. Owens," said the captain. "Fetch the gold piece in my quarters. It is time to reward the lookout who spotted that fine bull sperm two days hence."

A minute or two later, the first mate strolled across the deck and handed the shiny gold coin to the captain. "Step forward, mate, and claim your reward," shouted the captain as he struggled to rouse himself out of his melancholy state.

Death on the High Seas

Moments later, the keen-eyed lookout stepped forward and received his impressive reward.

"Now," began Captain Flynn, "I pledge two gold coins to the man who finds me Big Jack. Will ye drink with me, boys? Will ye drink to the death of old Jack? Mr. Owens," continued the captain, who by this point was in a fit of passion, "break out the full measure of grog!"

Shouts of approval quickly rang in the air, as the men prepared to partake of strong drink. For my part, I hardly saw the point in celebrating in this fashion, for strong drink never held any attraction for me. As I looked over in the direction of my friend, Shawn Hammer, it was evident that he was also disturbed by the whole scene.

"We must pull together, lads, as one man in our quest to kill old Jack," continued the captain. "All ye that are true whale men will not fail to drink from this jug. Come heaven or hell, men, we must not leave these waters until Jack spouts black blood and rolls over dead."

I was not sure who it was that addressed us from the main deck, for it was surely not the same Argus Flynn that sailed with us out of New Bedford. If I did not know better, I would certainly have concluded at that moment that Captain Flynn had gone mad. His very countenance and spirit was the picture of folly and darkness. The more I contemplated the whole attitude of our formerly levelheaded leader, the more my soul withdrew in fear.

As the jug of grog was passed to me, I was unable to summon the courage to pass it by as I had routinely done in the past. I, therefore, pretended to drink from the jug, to pacify the demands of Captain Flynn, and quickly handed it off to my friend Shawn Hammer. As the so-called celebration of unity continued, all eyes were fixed on my friend, as he stood motionless with the jug at his side.

"Drink deep and quickly, man!" shouted the captain in an agitated voice.

"Sir," responded my shipmate Shawn, "I have sworn an oath since my youth not to touch strong drink."

"Oh," said Argus Flynn, "are ye a Quaker boy, then?" hoping to humiliate the principled young sailor.

"No sir," stated Shawn. "But what I am is a man seeking to keep his word. When a man gives a pledge to his Maker, he should keep it. I will not judge you, Captain, in regard to meat and drink. All I ask is to be left alone to decide whether or not to partake of strong drink."

"Enough of this nonsense and babbling," asserted the captain rudely. "If I want to hear a sermon, boy, I will pay a visit to the Seaman's Bethel. As I size you up, I see someone who is afraid of becoming a true New Bedford man. Real whaling men, you should understand, never refuse to drink with their shipmates!"

"Strong drink is not the true measure of a man, Captain Flynn. In fact, more often than not, it is the ruin of him," replied the young sailor firmly.

"Go on then, pass the jug to the real whale man standing next to ye," concluded the captain in an angry tone.

I, for one, was sickened by the whole exchange between Argus Flynn and my friend Shawn. Perhaps what was more disheartening about the experience, however, was the discovery of how little moral courage I possessed within my soul. After the little celebration was over and we all returned to our duties, I tried to be particularly kind to my shipmate Shawn, for he was clearly downcast.

As I struggled to shake off the events of that evening, I was glad to spend some time alone in the bow of the *Landsman*. After much prayer and contemplation, I resolved to make a greater effort to live out my faith with the same courage as Shawn Hammer. In many respects, the hours that I spent staring at the waves and communing with the Lord were of immense spiritual benefit to me. As later events would reveal, God was strengthening me for even greater trials that He was about to send my way.

The next morning, after a hearty breakfast of oatmeal and biscuits, I walked over to the windlass and sat down on a large barrel located nearby. As I sat whistling a favorite tune, I watched five men who were in my vicinity. Some of the men were busy sharpening harpoons and cutting knives, while others were making all kinds of toys or gifts from their supply of whale bone.

After several minutes, I became somewhat restless and began to stroll about the deck in search of something to do. As I passed by a group of my shipmates, I heard one of them describing in mournful terms how the whale that he recently harpooned and killed sank to the bottom before it could be towed to the *Landsman*. Upon hearing this tale, I simply smiled to myself, for such disappointments were the common lot of a whale man.

One week passed, rather uneventfully, as our quest for the legendary whale continued. As might be expected, the talk among the men ranged from the change in the captain's attitude to that of who would win the coveted gold coins for spotting Big Jack. This particular day, being Sunday, Shawn Hammer and a few other men joined me early in the forenoon for a time of Bible reading and worship. As prayers were lifted up by each of the men in attendance, it was evident that all of us were concerned for the spiritual estate of Argus Flynn. Although the captain was commonly regarded as a decent man, he was not known to be a Christian or even a Sabbath keeper.

The longer we prayed and talked together after services, the more we became convinced of the goodness of God in placing us on a whaler that seldom required hard labor on the Sabbath. It should be known that whaling men, as a rule, do not concern themselves with spiritual things. Most whaling men, in other words, would never think of letting the Lord's Day interfere with their selfish ambitions. Besides which, it is the rule of the sea that the captain's orders must be obeyed, even if his orders may come on a Sunday.

Thankfully, no whales of any size were spotted on that Lord's Day, so the issue of going after whales on Sunday soon passed from our minds.

The new week opened on a hopeful note, as our crew spotted and killed two right whales and one sperm whale. Although the sperm whale was a modest sized creature, he was not to be compared to the two right whales, which fetched us almost sixty barrels each. For the first time in days, I actually saw Captain Flynn laugh with one of his officers. I was hopeful that this was a sign that he was beginning to recover from his melancholy state.

The remainder of this week was quiet as the crew busied itself with storing barrels in the hold and cleaning up the ship. During this same period, Captain Flynn sailed the *Landsman* over to the nearby port city of Cape Town, in order to secure needed provisions and fresh water. Only the anxiousness of our captain prevented us from receiving the liberty to go ashore at this place. After the shore party returned from the docks with our goods we, therefore, quickly stored these provisions in our hold, and set sail once again.

Before we knew it, it was the Lord's Day once again. After services, several men stood around telling stories of high sea adventure, mixed with a good dose of humor and malarkey. There are few things in life that a sailor loves more than a good story or yarn, and soon the *Landsman's* deck was filled with laughter.

All of a sudden, the man at the mast's head sang out that a large sperm whale was spouting away two points off the port bow. This call came as a particular surprise, for it had been many months since our crew had spotted any large whale on a Sunday

As usual, Captain Flynn rushed up to the main deck and yelled, "Is it Big Jack?"

"Can't say for sure, Captain," came the reply. "All I know is that it looks like a big sperm bull."

Without hesitation, Captain Flynn gave the order to ready the boats for lowering. As the thought never entered my mind to disobey a direct order, I went like the rest to my assigned post. As I was in the process of scrambling to get my gear assembled near the long boats, I noticed that Shawn Hammer was conversing with the first mate. This unexpected act, coupled with the rather animated gestures coming from Mr. Owens, caused me to wonder if something was amiss. After all, I knew very well that my friend Shawn was fit for duty, therefore, I could scarcely think of why he would not feel obliged to be at his station like the rest of us. As it turned out, I did not have to wait long to discover the source of this mystery, for I watched as Mr. Owens dragged my young friend over toward the captain and said:

"Beggin your pardon, sir, but seaman Hammer has just informed me that he is not inclined to assume his post, given the fact that this is Sunday. He requests permission to be relieved from his duty."

"Permission denied," stated the captain firmly. "And kindly remind this seaman that I am not running a pleasure cruise, and that I fully intend on holding him to the pledge he gave when he signed on to this crew to comply with all of my orders."

"May I have a word with you directly, sir?" asked the nervous seaman, as he touched his cap in the form of a salute.

"I have no time for words just now, Mr. Hammer, for I have work to do," added Argus Flynn. "It is enough for me to remind you of your duty and to insist upon your prompt compliance. Don't think for one moment lad that I will tolerate your insubordination. It may well be that you have a right not to drink grog aboard my ship; but as long as you are fit for duty, you will perform your common service as a whaleman regardless of the day of the week."

"Sir, I want to do the whole of my duty, and to do right by your command," replied the God-fearing sailor. "But especially since the Lord delivered me from a watery grave, but a short time ago, He has opened my eyes to recognize my need to obey His orders first and last. You see, …"

Before he could say another word, however, Captain Flynn ordered the first mate to seize my noble friend and place him in one of the long boats.

"If he resists, Mr. Owens, make it clear to our confused shipmate that he will be hung from the yardarm until the birds pick the flesh off of his miserable carcass," commanded Argus Flynn, with a voice that was loud enough for all to hear.

In less than one minute, Shawn Hammer was forcefully deposited into Mr. Owens whaling boat, as it hung at the davits. Having no choice in the matter, my humiliated friend resigned himself to God's will, and picked up his oar in the midst of a chorus of sneers and laughter.

"There she blows!" cried a voice from the masthead. "I saw her breech, Captain, two points off our lee beam. It's old Jack, for sure!"

With a gleam in his eye, the captain jumped in his boat, and roared: "Lower away, with all speed!"

As soon as our boats hit the water, all of the thoughts of the men quickly turned to the hunt. We were all keenly aware of the fact that each and every one of us was about to be engaged in a long and memorable battle. Each man, therefore, began to brace himself for the fight. Little did we know, however, that the events that would soon unfold would prove to be more dreadful than any of us could have imagined.

Upon receiving the order to pull, those of us at the oars moved instinctively to our task, and were soon in a good rhythm. As our craft began to glide across the gray ocean waves, gulls began to circle about us, sending out their usual chatter. Every effort was made to overtake the clever old bull named Jack, but after an hour of nearly constant rowing, we were still unable to come alongside him.

After almost a year at sea, I was finally beginning to recognize that no two hunts were ever quite the same. On some occasions, for example, we would come across large whale that appeared to be nothing less than a mighty leviathan; yet, when we chased him down, we found that he was not so tough after all. At other times, however, we would cross paths with a relatively small whale and find nothing but grief and hardship for our trouble. If there is one thing I learned well from the older men, it was never to take anything for granted while pursuing the monsters of the deep. Over and over again, I was told, 'Never turn your back on a whale, son, never!'

As we continued our quest to capture Big Jack, it soon became clear that he was the type of whale that would not surrender his life without a fight. I say this because the first two serious attempts that we made to engage him, ended up in failure, for he chased us off by trying to ram two of our boats with his scarred head. After several additional disappointments, Captain Flynn determined to employ a new strategy in his fight against old Jack.

Our leaders revised plan, emphasized the need for our three boats to work together in a more coordinated fashion. No longer would we simply chase this legendary whale and let our fastest boat try to get a single lance in him. Rather, we would pursue him from three separate directions at once. A brief conference was held, therefore, between the three officers who commanded our whaling boats in order to establish a clear plan of attack.

Nearly twenty minutes passed before our three boats were in their proper position and prepared to attack the clever giant from three directions. One boat, headed by Mr. Owens, was stationed in front of old Jack and would be the first to strike him head on. The other two boats, led by Argus Flynn and the second mate, would then attack the mighty sperm from both sides, moments after Mr. Owens and his crew had done their work. This bold plan, it should be mentioned, was also acknowledged to be a dangerous one; for if anything went wrong, our hunting party would not have any boat in reserve to rescue those in need.

Notwithstanding the dangers involved, each crew prepared to do its duty to the last man and the last boat. The opening of the battle was signaled, when a small flag was hoisted by the first mate. Moments later, we heard the word "Attack!" come from the mouths of Mr. Owens' crew. As we held our breath, we could see our brave comrades heading right for the jaws of old Jack. They had not traveled very far, however, before we saw the bull sperm dive straight under the ocean waves in their general direction.

At this critical point in the fight our leader, being blinded by impatience, signaled the other boats to close in with all possible speed.

"That old devil Jack may be clever, men," shouted Argus Flynn to those of us who were near him awaiting our next orders. "But we will be ready to strike him fore and aft when he rises! Forward, shipmates. Forward!"

With all of the strength we could muster, we pulled hard at our oars towards a whale that was still hidden under the waves. Before we had progressed very far, however, we saw what appeared to be a large gray object looming directly under Mr. Owens' boat. In an instant, our worst fears were realized, as a mountain of dark gray flesh suddenly exploded directly beneath this boat, sending men and equipment flying in all directions. Almost immediately, the air was filled with the cries of desperate men, and the sound of breaking timbers.

Much to the surprise of all of those manning the captain's boat, we heard him scream: "Now men, after him, we must avenge the insult done to our shipmates!"

"Sir," cried a sailor who sat near him, "What about the men in the water. We can't proceed without endangering their very lives."

"The men will be cared for in due time," replied the reckless leader. "Pull men, we must have that fish!"

Amidst the confusion and chaos, and with plenty of misgivings, we followed the urging of our captain and headed straight for the side of Big Jack. In less than a minute we were at the monster's side, and our harpooner immediately sent his weapon deep into the vitals of our adversary. Not surprisingly, however, the mighty creature reacted to this painful stabbing by throwing his flukes down upon the men who were still floating in the water just behind him. In a matter of seconds, we also recognized that the second mate had managed to hurl a harpoon deep into the opposite side of Big Jack. As it happened, these mortal wounds were delivered at almost the exact same moment, and resulted in the immediate death of this powerful creature. This was the true reason why our prey reacted so quickly and violently to the work of our harpooners.

The death march or flurry of old Jack soon began in earnest, therefore, as he swam about in a large circle and beat the ocean with his tail in a final act of defiance and rage. As this strange and tragic spectacle continued to play out under our watchful eye, we longed for the opportunity to row closer to where our surviving shipmates were floating in order to effect their rescue. As it turned out, however, the dangers that were posed by the final thrashing of the dying sperm made it quite impossible for us to get close enough to the men who so desperately needed our aid. Great was the anguish in our souls at that moment, as we were forced to sit at our oars and watch one after another of the men who had formerly occupied Mr. Owen's whaling boat be thrashed to death by the cruel and senseless tail of Big Jack. If I live to be a hundred, I can assure you that old Jim Surrey will never be able to forget that horrific scene.

By the time the giant sperm finally rolled over in death, we had precious few shipmates left to rescue, for no fewer than five men were lost during our protracted engagement. With great care and considerable weeping, we went about the grim task of rescuing the survivors, and retrieving the dead. By the mercy of God, Mr. Owens was numbered amongst the survivors, although he was severely bruised and battered. This bit of good news was quickly countered, however, by virtue of the fact that listed among the dead was none other than my close friend Shawn Hammer.

As I trust you will understand, all during the process of tying off our prize whale, as well as in our journey back to the *Landsman*, not one cheer was lifted up. In fact, one might say that our long and dreary trek back to our ship had more the air of a funeral procession, rather than a victory celebration. We had, indeed, killed a big whale that day, but the hearts of every one of us were heavy as we contemplated the great price that was paid to achieve such fleeting glory.

Chapter 12
A New Creature in Christ

The death of young Shawn Hammer, as well as the other four men, cast a gloom over the entire ship for a number of days. I could not help but notice, however, that Captain Flynn appeared to be impacted as much, if not more, than most by the deaths of those who were under his charge. For the first time during our voyage, our leader made a point of reading a portion of Holy Scripture at the gangway of our ship at the conclusion of the committal service for our slain comrades. After his remarks concluded, we dispatched the bodies of those who had perished over the side, in the usual sailor fashion. Each man was wrapped in his own hammock, with a cannon ball at his feet to sink him, and then cast into the deep while his shipmates watched in silence.

Several days after the committal service, I remember being called into the captain's quarters. Like most of the men, I had scarcely seen much of Argus Flynn for some time, so his invitation was as unexpected as it was welcome. It was late in the afternoon, when I stepped through the narrow door that led into the skipper's cabin. Upon entering his quarters, I removed my cap as a sign of respect.

"Greetings, Mr. Surrey," began the captain. "I suppose you may be wondering why I called you here."

"Well, I hope it is not due to any offense on my part, Captain," I replied.

"No, no, rest easy man," you are not under any discipline," he slowly remarked, as he stepped out of the shadows and revealed his rather dejected countenance. "I have called you here because you were quite close to one of the young men who was recently slain. The man we knew as Shawn Hammer."

"Yes, sir, I was about as close to Shawn as two men can get in regards to friendship and all. We shared much in common as messmates, but the true strength of our friendship flowed out of our common faith in Jesus Christ."

"Now that you mention it, Jim," responded the captain, "that is precisely why I have called you to my quarters. I have spent the last week in great inner conflict and turmoil, trying to sort out where I stand in regard to the Almighty. I have never been a very religious man as you know, and yet, now I find that my spirit is broken and I don't know how to effect its repair. I simply can't walk away from the fact that my rash actions may well have contributed to the death of five good men. I am convinced, in truth, that God is tormenting me on account of the damage that I caused to the bodies and souls of these sailors."

"And so, you have called me alongside you now to help in some degree to lessen your burden. Is that it?"

"I suppose that is it," remarked the confused sinner named Argus. "Can you not help me in some manner, for no matter what I do, my guilt does not seem to be lessened in the slightest? Perhaps I just need to try harder to be a better man; perhaps then I can begin to atone for my misdeeds. I have tried to read the Bible, and to pray for forgiveness, but ..."

"But you have no heart for the business of repentance, which you know full well the Lord requires of you. You insist, in fact, on coming to God on your own terms, and in your own assumed righteousness. The conflicts and burdens that are weighing down your heart at this hour, captain, stem solely from the weight of sin that now wars against your spirit and keeps you in bondage to your own sinful nature. You feel as though you are powerless to overcome this burden, for the simple reason that God is now graciously permitting you to see your true condition. The plain truth, dear man, is that you are a lost and helpless slave of sin, with a heart that is alienated from its Maker."

"So, there is no hope for me. Is that your message?" replied the captain, in a despondent tone of voice.

A New Creature in Christ

"If left to your self, yes," came the reply. "But, the good news for any sinner or lost soul, is that you have a true champion and burden bearer standing close at hand. His name is Jesus Christ, and He is able to save to the uttermost all those who come to Him in simple child-like faith. Come to the Savior now captain, without delay, for His blood and righteousness alone can wash away your sins. Seek the Lord while He may be found, for he is strong to save, and you will find at last an anchor for your soul that is sure and steadfast."

"Will you stay with me awhile to pray, Jim? I am rather new to this business of speaking to God."

"I would be honored to lead you to the throne of grace, dear friend; but I want to encourage you to rest in the promise of Scripture that declares that God's arms are open to those who approach Him with a contrite heart. In the book of Matthew, chapter eleven, we read: 'Come unto Me, all ye that labour and are heavy laden, and I will give you rest. Take my yoke upon you, and learn of me; for I am meek and lowly of heart: and ye shall find rest unto your souls.' And again, in the book of First John, chapter one, we are told: 'If we confess our sins, he is faithful and just to forgive us our sins, and to cleanse us from all unrighteousness.'"

So, under the dim light that shone from Captain Flynn's lantern, we knelt together as friends and poured out our petitions and supplications to Almighty God. As I rose to leave his cabin several minutes later, I am pleased to tell you that the tears that sat upon the rugged cheeks of Argus Flynn were that of joy, and not of sorrow.

Not long after my meeting with the captain, life aboard the *Landsman* slowly began to return to a more normal routine. After several days of living in the shadows and gloom, it was a welcome relief to many on board to be able to pour themselves into their work. The men that were lost would never be completely forgotten by those of us who remained alive; but a sailor's life at sea is one of constant challenge and duty, therefore, he cannot afford to allow the sorrows of his heart to sit long upon his mind. For this reason, after several days of mourning, each man on board began to try to move past his grief and carry on with his work.

Whales soon began to appear around us as we started our long journey back to New Bedford. The now familiar cry of "There she blows!" rang out frequently as the weeks past. Each time, we would hear the steady voice of the captain cry, "Where away?" and then, "Lower away." Then came the chase with all its dangers and excitement, followed by the striking of the mighty whale until, at last, it floated calmly on the sea.

During this time period, for reasons already explained, we all threw ourselves into our work in an effort to try to forget those who were no longer swinging in their hammocks. But, in spite of our best efforts, the hearts of one and all were not as light as before. Although none of us tried to show it, I knew full well that many a laugh was checked and many a joke was repressed, for the memory of our dead shipmates.

The sailor who continued to be most affected by the loss of our comrades, however, was the captain. This was natural and did not surprise us, but we were not prepared for the great change that soon appeared in his manner and conduct. After a time, he laughed with the rest of us at a good joke and cheered loudly when a big whale turned belly up. But his behavior toward us was more considerate and fatherly, and he entirely abandoned the habit of swearing. He also began to try to honor the Lord by respecting the Christian Sabbath. Many a whale did I see sporting and spouting near us on that day, but never again after the death of our shipmates did we lower a boat or touch a harpoon on Sunday.

A few of the unsaved sailors on board used to swear against his policy and complain of it to each other. Yet, these men never had the courage of their convictions to voice their concerns directly to the captain, and they soon gave up their grumbling, when the rest of us reminded them that they had agreed to it when the captain first proposed the idea.

I well remember that it was the second Sunday after Shawn's death, when the captain assembled our crew on the quarterdeck and spoke to us about his desire to limit our work on the Sabbath.

"Men," said Captain Flynn, "I've called you aft to make a proposal that may perhaps surprise you. Up to this point in

A New Creature in Christ

our voyage, as you know right well, I have not directed us to keep the Christian Sabbath with any consistency. Since our shipmate Shawn died, however, I have been thinkin' much on this matter. I've come to the conclusion that we should rest from all work on the Lord's Day, except those works that are necessary to keep the ship safe and sound. Now, men, I will not try to pretend that I am a wise theologian who has worked out exactly how the Sabbath should be kept, and to what degree the Christian Sabbath is binding upon men today. This I do know, shipmates, that in times past I have neglected and despised my Maker, and in time to come I mean to try to honor Him and obey His commandments. Well, what say ye, men? Shall we give the whales a rest on Sunday?"

We all agreed to this proposal at once, for the effect of the captain's speech was great upon the entire crew. It was not so much what he said, as the earnest and heartfelt way in which he said it. When our bold and manly captain, who never flinched from danger or duty, began to speak tenderly of his love for Jesus Christ, it was difficult for many of the sailors to believe their ears.

This was the final word from the captain about this matter, but in the days that followed, various members of the crew had many a hot discussion in the forecastle about this issue. Some men were in favor of the new move, and quickly defended the captain, while others called the captain an old woman and warned that our ship would never reach its quota.

In the course of time, however, we began to notice some very real benefits associated with the captain's new policy. Strengthened in body and spirit by resting one day, we possessed a greater vigor as we pursued our work the other six days. In our renewed strength we soon killed a number of whales under difficult circumstances, without losing one to the bottom of the ocean. The blessing of the Almighty could also be noted in that the general health of the crew improved, and we had far fewer injuries or accidents. I firmly believe, that all of these blessings were the direct result of God's promise to bless those who "call the Sabbath a delight, the holy of the Lord, honorable." (Isaiah 58:13)

One of the most memorable events in the entire voyage was the day that the captain celebrated God's goodness in helping us to fill our ship's hold with oil much sooner than expected. During this special celebration, the men who had been grumbling came forward and freely admitted that their concerns had been baseless. The crowning event of the day, however, was when the ship's carpenter nailed a beautifully carved wooden plaque over the captain's quarters, which stated: "Them that honor Me, I will honor."

As a result of all these events, any member of our crew that had the slightest spiritual interest soon became accustomed to looking for a blessing on the Sabbath. Obviously, however, the captain tried to remind the crew that the true purpose for obeying any of God's commandments was not to obtain some specific temporal blessing, but to lay up spiritual treasures in heaven.

Although many changes had taken place aboard the *Landsman* since it first set sail, particularly since Argus Flynn had come to faith in Christ, my weekly assignment as a lookout at the masthead had not been altered. For some strange reason, perhaps because of my keen eyesight, the captain made a point of keeping me posted in the crow's nest on a regular basis.

I well remember the time, shortly after we had begun our homeward bound journey, when I made a discovery from my lookout platform that was truly extraordinary. It was on a warm autumn day in the year of our Lord 1847, as I scanned the horizon looking for big whales, that I noticed a faint object appear in the distance. At first, I was not at all confident that I could even properly identify the tiny object that was floating on the surface. The faint outline suggested that it might be a single large whale, or perhaps a small boat.

As the minutes past, I began to doubt that it could, indeed, be a stray boat for there was no whaling bark or schooner anywhere in view. Nevertheless, I was soon forced to re-evaluate my assumptions when the object came closer to our bark, and I noticed a white distress flag being waved from the center of a lone long boat. Once I had made positive identification of the

A New Creature in Christ 113

craft, I shouted, "Boat ahoy!" to the officer who was posted on the main deck.

In a matter of moments, the second mate called up to me and asked, "Where away?"

"Four points off the port bow, sir. I make it to be a single long boat," I replied.

While I was still in the act of looking down, I noticed that Captain Flynn had decided to come on deck in order to look at our unexpected visitor through his looking glass. "My word, Mr. Surrey, you certainly have the eyes of a hawk," remarked the skipper. "I can hardly make them out with the aid of my glass!"

After the captain finished his remarks, he ordered the helmsman to steer a course in order to intercept the whaling boat that appeared to be floating aimlessly on the sea. As the *Landsman* crept closer to the long boat, I was finally in the position to give the captain a few more details. For this reason, I shouted, "There looks to be five men aboard, sir, and at least one of them appears to be injured."

"Very well, Mr. Surrey," he responded, before adding: "We should come alongside her in short order. Clew up the main sails, and make all preparations to take on boarders."

In less than two minutes, I saw one of the men in the long boat slowly stand up to receive the line that was in the process of being tossed to him from our crew. With some difficulty, he finally managed to grab this line and pull himself and his shipmates alongside of our bark.

The injured man was the first sailor to be helped aboard, and then, the remainder of the lost souls soon followed. It was immediately evident that the wounded sailor was in considerable pain. The rest of his shipmates, however, also looked rather rough around the edges. Only after our cook gave these pathetic looking creatures a mug of cider and a biscuit, did they seem to show signs of coming around.

As we sat and stared at our uninvited guests, our captain eventually got around to asking these men to tell their story.

"First off," began their leader, "we are grateful to be delivered from that cramped and soggy boat, and from what would have likely been a slow death by starvation. We are whaling men from the bark *Wanderer*, outward bound from the port of New Bedford. Three days ago, while on a routine hunt, we struck a large bull in these waters that gave us quite a stir and pulled us far away from our ship. At the end of it all, one of our shipmates was injured and we were forced to cut loose from our fish. By the time we finally realized how far we had strayed, a dense fog suddenly arose, and we were unable to find our ship through the growing darkness. We then tried for the better part of two days to locate our ship, but our efforts did not meet with success. Yours was the first and only vessel to cross our path since our calamity first set in. We have spent the last two nights in this open boat, with little food and no water."

"Tell me what you can of the condition of your men," requested Argus Flynn, as he motioned for the cook to dispense fresh water to the five men who had recently come on board.

"I am rather certain that the man you first helped aboard has three broken ribs, two cracked teeth, and a broken nose. The rest of us are badly bruised, and suffering from exposure, but otherwise fit for duty."

"Well," replied our skipper to the weary guests, "after your injuries are addressed you will, of course, be free to sail away to resume your search for the *Wanderer*. On the other hand, you may also choose to stay aboard my ship until we dock once more in New Bedford town. Regardless of your decision, be assured that we will extend to you the right arm of Christian hospitality while you are among us."

"Much obliged, sir," came the reply from the rescued sailor. "We will give you our answer by the morning light."

The following morning, the five whaling men that we had rescued informed Argus Flynn that they would sign on as shipmates aboard the *Landsman* for the remainder of our voyage.

"Your home is our home, captain, therefore your ship is our ship," stated the leader of the new recruits. "It would be sheer folly to try to set out in that long boat again on the faint chance of catching up to the *Wanderer*. Besides, at the end of the day, we are all New Bedford men."

A New Creature in Christ

"As captain, I receive you into our number with the firm belief that this is God's will. I would have you understand straight off men, that although I can not promise you a large share in the profits we gain from our voyage, this is still a working ship. We cannot abide freeloaders aboard the *Landsman*. You will have, therefore, your daily chores just like the other men. Mr. Owens, see to it that these men are situated below, and mark out for them the scope of their duties. Mr. Billings, set a course for the north and west."

"Thank you, sir," stated one of the new volunteers, "we will endeavor to pull our own weight as we are able, so that in time we can earn our salt. Oh, I almost forgot. The one man from our group who has the broken teeth is in need of a dentist sooner rather than later. Have you anyone on board that can help in this regard?"

"Seaman Surrey generally helps with such needs, but I believe that he broke his only pair of pliers while working on his last patient. All things considered, it may be best for your mate to look up the ship's carpenter. He seems to have the knack when it comes to pulling teeth, and I believe he has a pair of pliers that is suitable to the task."

So, what was loss to the captain of the *Wanderer*, was gain to the *Landsman*, as we enlisted five more souls to our crew. Now that I recall this situation further, however, I seem to remember that not everyone was equally thrilled with the arrival of these new shipmates. Our chief cook, who seldom seemed to be in a cheery mood even in the best of circumstances, summarized well the feelings of some as he said: "Just what I need, five more mouths to feed!"

A new type of excitement soon began to blossom on board the *Landsman*, as the weeks flew by quickly and the men started to think about being reunited with family and friends. Although in some ways it was hard to believe, our voyage was rapidly drawing to a close, and the overall mood and tempo of the ship slowly began to reflect this reality. The sometimes tense and strict relationship that existed between the officers and common seamen, for example, became more relaxed. As each day went by, even my songs became more focused upon the theme of returning home, in an attempt to keep the spirits of the men high.

More and more, the talk aboard the *Landsman* turned to the subject of what changes may have taken place in the world since we all left civilization. One day, as a group of officers were playing checkers on the main deck, the lookout shouted:

"Sail ho! Tall ship off the port bow, sir. Looks to be a whaler of some kind, about two miles out."

As Captain Flynn came up on deck, one of the officers asked, "Sir, it looks like the bark *Superior*, likely under the command of Captain James Royce is heading our way. Can we signal for a gam, sir?"

The captain thought on the idea for several moments, while he slowly sipped his coffee, sweetened with molasses. Finally, he responded, "Order the gam signal to be raised to the view of Captain Royce, and we shall see if he responds in kind."

A minute or two later, a signal flag was raised on the rigging of the *Superior* affirming their interest in participating in a gam.

"Square the yards. Look alive, my hearties!" yelled Captain Flynn, as he sought to slow the *Landsman's* movement through the sea. Within a short period of time, our bark was settling down nicely in the water in preparation for dropping anchor.

CHAPTER 13
A Gam Brings News from Home

The sound of bells soon filled the air, as Captain Flynn called all hands to the main deck. He thanked the crew for their hard work, and mentioned that he had decided to celebrate their accomplishments by giving them a chance to get together with some of the crew of the *Superior*.

"Hurrah, hurrah!" shouted the rowdy shipmates, as they reacted to the captain's words. Twenty-two months at sea had created a hunger in the crew for fresh news from other seamen.

"Where does the *Superior* hail from, Captain?" questioned the second mate.

"She is out of Sag Harbor, and her captain trained with me years ago in Nantucket," answered Argus Flynn. Moments later he added, "The last time I shipped out with James Royce was when we sailed on his bark up the Bering Sea, and hunted bowhead whales in the chilly Arctic waters. Worst backgammon player I ever knew."

Mr. Owens, who was standing nearby, stated: "If it's outward bound that she be then, Captain, chances are that these sailors will be able to give us fresh news from home. They probably just left New England about a fortnight ago."

"Well, it may be your hopes of fresh news will be realized, Mr. Owens," responded the captain. "But I should think that they have been outward bound for longer than a fortnight."

The sound of seagulls interrupted the closing words of Argus Flynn, as the crew eagerly awaited word about who would join the captain in his long boat journey over to the *Superior*, which was anchored nearby.

"Mr. Owens," called the captain, "let the men draw sticks to see who is to join me on my trip over to Captain Royce. The six men who draw the shortest sticks will accompany me."

"Aye, aye, sir," responded the first mate.

Several minutes later, a half-dozen men with smiling faces, including myself, came strolling up to the gangway and prepared for the order to get into the captain's boat.

"Take to your oars, men, and prepare to lower away," called the captain as he turned to his first mate. "You are in charge in my absence, Mr. Owens, so look well to your duty. Set the watch with diligence, and signal me at the first sign of trouble or foul weather."

"I will take good care of the *Landsman* and her crew until your return, Captain," the first mate assured him.

Before long, the captain and his picked crew were pulling their way across the water toward the neighboring ship. It only took about five minutes for us to row the short distance over to the *Superior*.

A Gam Brings News from Home

As we approached Captain Royce's bark, Argus Flynn softly said, "Ship your oars, men, and prepare to secure the bow line."

One of the sailors from the *Superior* suddenly leaned over the side and yelled: "Can I throw ye a line, sir?"

"Aye, mate," called Captain Flynn. "Ye better fit us out with two lines, fore and aft, for the wind is contrary and the sea is a might choppy."

"Very well, Captain Flynn," confirmed the young sailor.

After the boat was secured, Captain Flynn climbed up the side of the ship and pulled himself through the gangway that led to the main deck. As soon as his feet hit the hard and level deck, he called out loud and clear: "Requesting permission from the officer in charge to come aboard."

"Permission granted," uttered James Royce, as he finished walking over to the place where Captain Flynn had just climbed aboard his ship.

"Why, you old sea dog, how are you this fine day?" questioned the newly arrived guest.

"Never better, my old shipmate," came the quick response. "But before we go any further, I have need to ask: What are ye here for, Captain?"

Without hesitation, Captain Flynn recited the traditional response of whalemen. "I'm here for whales, oil, and hard work."

"Very well then, Captain. Ye be welcome aboard this whaler," said James Royce with a broad grin.

After a lively handshake between the two captains, James Royce gave the order for his first mate to take a group of sailors from the *Superior* to the *Landsman*. A short time later, Captain Royce yelled over in the direction of the galley. "Look lively now, cook. Our guests need their ration of plum duff and coffee."

As the captains continued to enjoy the process of getting reacquainted, the common sailors began to exchange stories, as well as books and newspapers. It was not long before I turned the discussion to the topic of recent events in New England. "What news have ye about old New Bedford town?" I asked.

One of the sailors from the *Superior* quickly responded, "Ye ought to know that New Bedford town seldom offers up fresh news of any kind, unless you consider reports of lost ships or sailors newsworthy. The talk of New England at this time, is the ending of the Mexican War by a treaty that is soon to be signed. It looks like our country may gain control over the territories of California and New Mexico as a result of the victories that have been won."

"What do you mean, we won the war in Mexico?" I asked. "I did not even know that our country was in a war south of the border. We shipped out in the early part of 1846."

My shipmate, Ben Lodins, continued the discussion by asking, "What other details can you share with us about this war?"

"Well," mentioned another sailor, "our fighting men under General Scott managed to storm Mexico City in the fall, and the Mexican government sued for peace. Not all of the citizens of New England, however, were happy about our victory. The famous author, Henry David Thoreau, from Massachusetts, is speaking out against the war. He claims that the conflict is more about extending slavery than anything else. In fact, Mr. Thoreau recently spent a night in jail due to his refusal to pay a poll tax to help pay for the recent war in Mexico."

"And how about some of the new inventions?" I questioned. "Has Samuel Morse done anything more with that talking wire telegraph he demonstrated a few years back?"

"Precious little," responded one of the officers from Captain Royce's ship. "It's not clear whether Morse's magic wire will get much use in New England, but, according to the newspapers, he remains hopeful."

As the sun rose higher in the sky, the atmosphere aboard the *Superior* became increasingly jovial. While new friendships were being made, the cook finally appeared on deck with mugs of plum pudding and a batch of rice cakes. It did not take long for us to devour these special treats.

A Gam Brings News from Home

While our second mate was in the middle of a humorous yarn, Captain Royce ordered all hands to come to the foredeck. As we stood around waiting for the captain's words, we soon heard him shout, "I want every soul on board to know that I am officially challenging Captain Flynn to a game of backgammon!"

"Oh, for the love of whales," groaned Argus Flynn.

"The loser of this contest between captains," continued James Royce, "will be obliged to shine the shoes of every sailor on board the *Superior*."

"Hurrah, hurrah!" bellowed the men, with gusto.

"Very well, very well," agreed Captain Flynn, who then added, "you have not beaten me in any previous contest, but I suppose there is a first time for everything."

A hush fell over the deck, as the two men began their all important contest. For the next two hours, all you could hear was the munching of rice cakes and the snickering of various members of the assembly. Finally, after the sun had begun to set, a simple question could be heard rising from the deck of the *Superior*. Captain Flynn asked his opponent, "So, when can I expect to see you take up your old hobby of shining boots, Captain?"

"All in good time, my ungracious guest," came the reply. "You would think after all these years that I would take up another game, but I must first find a way to beat you, at least once."

"Well, I admire your determination," said Captain Flynn, "but I think you would be better off using your determination for whaling, instead of backgammon."

The next instant, several of the men began to join me in singing a well known chantey, much to the satisfaction of Captain Royce. As the evening wore on, the air became filled with a steady stream of rowdy songs and hilarious stories. Only fatigue prevented our gam from continuing on past the midnight hour.

As the men prepared to settle into their bunks, Captain Royce gave his orders to those on watch and headed for his quarters. Captain Flynn crawled into the bunk normally occupied by the first mate, and was soon fast asleep.

The next morning dawned brightly, as the second watch of the day took their positions aloft. The breeze had slackened over the hours of the night, and we were all enjoying fair weather and warm hospitality.

As Captain Flynn walked the deck, he soon came across the path of his former backgammon rival. After a brief smile, he began, "Good morning, your excellency, how has your shoe shining been progressing?"

"Well enough, my curious friend," came the reply. "So when are you going to tell me about how your whaling game has gone these past two years?" added Captain Royce.

"The Almighty has been gracious to us, very gracious," began the captain in a sincere tone. "We have filled our hold to capacity slightly ahead of schedule. I would have you know, however, that our voyage has been attended by hardships, as well as by blessings. In the providence of God, we lost a total of six sailors to this point in our journey. The good Lord has recently seen fit to permit us to rescue five lost souls who were adrift on the high seas, however, thus restoring to us nearly our full compliment of men."

"I see," responded Captain Royce. "When are you hoping to reach New Bedford?"

"My plan is to make sail this afternoon, with the hope of reaching port in about two weeks. Do you think we can reach home in this time, if the winds are favorable?"

"Quite likely, Captain," responded James Royce, "but we will miss out on the opportunity to finish our next round of backgammon."

"Lord willing, we can take care of that detail when we meet again. In the meantime, you have big whales to catch and blubber to process," concluded Captain Flynn.

"True enough, my old friend," said the captain of the *Superior*.

A Gam Brings News from Home

An hour or two later, Argus Flynn could be heard saying, "Prepare our boat for launch, men. Stow your gear and be ready on my order."

We all nodded in recognition of the captain, but in truth, none of us wanted the gam to end so soon. The two captains bid each other farewell and Godspeed amidst a carefully concealed veil of tears. Before we left the *Superior*, however, our skipper presented a special gift to James Royce in recognition of his hospitality. As Captain Royce began to open his gift, a rising tide of laughter soon broke forth on board, for the present was a new kit for shining shoes.

As the wind began to stiffen, we quickly completed our final preparations for getting underway. Upon the order of Captain Flynn, we soon found ourselves dipping our oars in the water in an effort to get back to our ship. On our way back, we met the men from the *Superior* who had just completed their gam on the *Landsman*. As our boats passed each other amidships, each crew let out a parting cheer and continued on its way with a light heart.

Chapter 14
Home at Last

As we prepared to take the *Landsman* on the final leg of her homeward bound journey, several men were sent into the rigging to put more canvas aloft. The first mate also began to busy himself with the task of organizing groups of men who would be responsible for cleaning certain areas of the ship. After almost two years at sea, it was universally acknowledged that the *Landsman* clearly needed some sprucing up.

During the latter part of the day, after we had gotten underway, the captain made a point of visiting with each work party to inspect its progress. "Make her shine, lads. The owners expect me to return their boat in good order," remarked the seasoned skipper. "Mr. Owens," he continued, "I am going to my cabin to work on my log and journal. Trim the sails and set our course for home."

"Aye, sir," answered the first mate.

As I finished waxing the area near the helm, I asked Mr. Owens why a captain needed to keep a logbook. He thought for a few moments and then responded, "Shipmate, a captain must give an account of his gains to those he is working for. A captain must keep an accurate tally of the number of barrels of oil on board, the type of whales that were captured and the location in which each whale was taken. These records not only enable the owners to clearly see how their ship performed at sea, but can also provide invaluable information by which future voyages can be governed. Whales, as ye know, tend to be creatures of habit, and often swim in the same waters year after year."

Before long, it was evening on board the *Landsman*, as many of the sailors busied themselves by making final preparations for arriving in New Bedford. Most of the men took to having their hair cut, and some even went so far as to bathe with soap. As the evening meal was being passed out, I determined to get caught up with the mending of my jacket and pants. After my efforts were completed, however, it reminded me of just how much I missed my dear mother.

Unlike the early months at sea, I seldom thought of my mother unless some circumstance would spark my memory. Now that we were just days away from port, however, my mind began, once again, to think about her. Was she prospering? Did she survive the lonely nights with a stout heart? As I thought on these things, I comforted my heart with the knowledge that I would soon know the answer to these questions.

Before going on watch, Ben Lodins came up to me and asked, "So how are ye going to spend your share of money, Jim?"

Never having given it much thought, I said, "The first part of my money will go to paying for those who took care of my widowed mother these two years. Whatever is left over, I hope to use in the purchase of a piece of land for myself."

"Just be careful of land sharks," warned my shipmate, wryly.

"What are land sharks, if ye don't mind me askin'?" said I, with a strange expression on my face.

"Why, they are clever salesmen sent out by the merchants and outfitters in town. Their sole duty is to persuade you to purchase something substantial on the spur of the moment, before you can get your wits about you. They may also try to get you to sign on for another whaling voyage in a rash manner."

"Oh, I see," was my response. "Thanks for the tip, mate. I will do my level best to steer clear of those vermin."

After I completed my so-called "dogwatch", which lasted well past midnight, I retired to my bunk and quickly fell asleep. Six hours later, I awoke from a restless sleep to the sound of a hymn. Much to my surprise, the captain had decided to join with a few of the men in a rousing chorus of *Blest Be the Tie That Binds*. As I finished dressing, the sweet sounds of a familiar song of praise were soon replaced by the gravely voice of the second mate, who shouted, "All hands on deck!"

Home at Last

I quickly made my way topside and joined the men who were gathered together toward the stern of the ship. Moments later, Captain Flynn proceeded to fulfill his pledge by awarding the sailor who was responsible for spotting Big Jack with two gold coins.

As this middle-aged sailor examined his treasure, he smiled so hard that I thought that his face would break. Before dismissing the assembly, Argus Flynn added, "Men, our journey is almost over. We have all learned many things as we have sailed together and faced dangers of every sort. Our battle with whales may be over at this stage of our voyage, but we still have to fight against our sinful natures. Let us finish our voyage, therefore, with diligence and integrity, and ask the Almighty to guide us safely home to our loved ones. For your safety, I have ordered Mr. Owens to double the watch so as to keep a sharp eye out for rocks. I expect you all to cooperate with this order. Return to your posts, men."

The next three days at sea were cloudy and windy. It was only with great difficulty that the helmsman was able to keep the *Landsman* fairly on course. The following day, however, dawned clear and calm, as seagulls began to hover close to our whaler. As we began to move closer to the coast of New England, our lookouts began to spot an increasing number of small fishing vessels, in addition to outbound whalers of every sort. All of these sights and sounds served to boost the expectation that each man on board had that New Bedford was near. No longer did the officers need to require men to stand watch, for nearly every seaman on board was stationed somewhere along the perimeter of the *Landsman*, eagerly scanning the horizon.

Finally, after what seemed like an eternity, the lookout bellowed, "Land ho!"

The first landmass that we spotted was the familiar island of Nantucket. A short time later, we passed Martha's Vineyard. Captain Flynn then ordered our final turn toward the harbor of New Bedford. As the grand old lighthouse, which stood prominently in the harbor, came clearly into view, our hearts began to beat with greater intensity.

It was not long before we could begin to see the two-story mansions, which towered above the wharf. For several generations, the wives of New Bedford stood watch for incoming vessels from small platforms, which were perched atop these tall mansions. More than anything, those wives wished to be the first to know if they would be a happy whale man's wife or a widow. For this reason, the small rooftop decks were commonly called widow walks.

Home at Last

As the *Landsman* slipped into the main body of the harbor, the captain ordered all sails to be taken in. He then ordered all hands to prepare the ship for docking. As the *Landsman* began to be prepared for a well-deserved rest, crowds could be seen rushing to the waterfront. News had spread through town that Captain Flynn's bark had appeared in the harbor, and, as usual, such a report generated excitement.

After our beloved ship was tied fast to the dock, Captain Flynn took several minutes to say farewell to the men under his command. I well remember the words that were exchanged between us that day, as he came before me. We began with a hearty hug, and then I asked, "Well, Captain, it has been a voyage I will never forget. It does not seem possible that our task is at an end. What will you do now, sir?"

"As captain of this ship, I still have one unfinished piece of business to take care of," asserted Argus Flynn soberly. "It is my duty to make contact with Shawn Hammer's mother so as to inform her of the fate of her son."

"Would you like me to join you, Captain?" I asked.

"No, mate," he said. "This is one job that belongs to me alone. Pray that I will have the courage to tell her the whole truth."

"Very well, Captain," I said. "Until we meet again, may the Lord bless you and keep you in the palm of His hand."

Several minutes passed before I could gather up the remainder of my gear and make my way to shore. When I finally reached the wharf, I was somewhat surprised by the fact that my mother was absent from those standing amidst the crowd. As I continued to walk up Water Street with my shipmate, Tim Dronner, he suddenly stopped and turned in my direction.

"What's the matter?" I asked.

"I almost forgot," he began. "A messenger stopped me a few minutes ago when we came ashore and gave me this note. It is addressed to you, Jim."

"So it is," I responded. "I wonder what it is about."

"In these situations, mate, you generally don't know until you open the letter and read it!"

"I suppose you are right, Tim. You always were the one with the sharp mind," I replied.

"Before you get any older, then, please open the note!" said Tim, with an impatient voice.

Tim stared at me as I quickly read the note, and then he asked, "Well, now what does it say?"

"It directs me to go promptly to the Seaman's Bethel upon my arrival. Strange, though, for it gives no further explanation."

"I hope everything is alright with your mother, shipmate," said Tim tenderly. "Do you want me to go with you?"

"No thanks, friend," said I, "for whatever the situation may be I am sure that Reverend Carlson can help me sort it out."

Amidst tears and hugs, Tim and I went our separate ways. It was difficult to part with a shipmate after so long of a journey together. Nevertheless, the afternoon was coming on and I needed to try to locate my mother and discover her true condition.

It seemed strange to be treading the streets of New Bedford once again. Thankfully, however, it did not take long for me to get my bearings and locate the correct path to the Seaman's Bethel. On my way up to Johnnycake Hill, I stopped at a store on Union Street to pick up an apple and a bag of nuts to munch on. I had not eaten in hours and it had been months since I had tasted fresh fruit of any kind. These simple items seemed like great luxuries to me, as did the taste of fresh water, for such things were often hard to come by at sea.

After my pint-sized meal was finished, I proceeded to the parsonage of Rev. Carlson. Numerous thoughts began to flood my mind as I approached the residence of my friend and pastor. Was my mother safe in Fairhaven, or was she ill and boarding in New Bedford? Was my mother even alive at all? I wondered. If she were safe and well, how would I get a ride over to see her? As I continued to ponder these questions, I walked up to the parsonage and knocked on the front door.

A few moments passed before the door began to swing open. I was both shocked and pleased to see that the woman who stood before me was none other than my mother. Shouts of joy soon could be heard in every direction, as my mother embraced me as only a mother can. She then spoke to me, saying, "My, how you have grown into manhood, my dear son, since you sailed away. You are, indeed, a sight for sore eyes."

"I, I, did not expect to see you here and now, Mother," I said in a stammering fashion. "But it is grand to be able to see you straight off, without having to hitch a ride out to your home in Fairhaven."

"Well, you might as well know, now, that I no longer live in Fairhaven," stated my mother directly.

"Oh, Mother, are things unwell?" I questioned. "Did you lose the old homestead?"

"There is no cause for alarm, my son; although our old home is gone things are very well, indeed."

As my mother was finishing her mystifying statement, Rev. Carlson made his appearance at the door. "Woman," he said, "don't you think it would be proper to invite your long lost son into his new home before he gets any more confused by your remarks?"

"New home, no longer live in Fairhaven?" I muttered. "Would someone kindly tell me what is going on?"

"All in good time, James, please come in and sit yourself down," urged the kindly parson. "It is a little difficult to know where to begin telling you of how things are at present. So much has changed, James, since you sailed away on Captain Flynn's bark."

"Well, for starters," I said, "what kind of care did you give my poor widowed mother in my absence that would cause her to lose her home. When I was here last, at least she had a roof over her head."

"Your mother has received the best care of any woman in New England, of that you can be certain. In regard to her having a roof over her head, I guess it might be most fitting to say that she simply exchanged her old roof for a new one. You see, James," said the preacher, "your mother and I are now married and living under the same roof."

"You mean to tell me, that my mother is your wife?" I said while scratching my head.

"Yes, James," he responded with a grin. "And it would also stand to reason that I would be your new father, if you will have me. Spending time with your mother caused me, in the providence of God, to grow in my admiration and affection for her many excellent qualities."

After a few seconds of thought, I stated, "If I can trust you as a temporary caregiver, there seems to be no reason for me not to trust you as a permanent one. By the look of contentment on my mother's face, it surely seems that you must have been giving her lots of loving care."

"Indeed he has," remarked my mother, "there were times after your father passed away, James, when I thought that I may never find a suitable man to fill his shoes. Thank God that my thinking was wrong. I have learned, once again, never to underestimate the power of the Almighty."

"So, how long has it been since you tied the bands?" I asked.

"Very nearly ten months, James," answered my newly discovered stepfather. "It is like I have always told you, God works in mysterious ways, His wonders to perform."

"Obviously, I regret not being here for the wedding ceremony," I added. "Yet it is a comfort knowing that my mother will be well cared for should I ever decide to seek my fortune at sea in the days ahead."

"At least, I hope that you will stick around our home long enough to let us fatten you up a bit before you venture out on another ship," pleaded my mother.

"I will try my level best to ignore the call of the sea for as long as possible, dear madam. Yet, I hasten to add that now that my passion has been stirred for high sea adventure it can only be but a brief season before I again go hunting for whales."

Home at Last

© Designpics, Inc.

CHAPTER 15
Old Glory and New Dreams

"So that is how my first voyage to the South Seas ended. As you might expect, in later years, Tim and I made many more trips as whaling men, both in the north and south. But I have already tried your patience, dear townsfolk, in being so long winded about my first adventure as a whaleman. I will, therefore, spare you from having to listen to any more stories about the bygone days of whaling.

"This more I will only say, that my life as a whaleman brought me into many dangers, but the Lord has preserved me safe through them all. Yea, and further still, He has preserved my soul in the midst of trials of a far worse kind than one's body falls in with while fighting whales."

The little group that had been listening to me so attentively for several hours seemed to suddenly come alive with questions. One young man finally summoned the courage to ask, "Why has whaling gone away from New Bedford? Are most of the whales gone from the seas?"

I pondered these questions for several moments, and then answered: "New Bedford's greatest year for whaling was 1857. At this time, during the glory days, ten thousand men were making their living in the whaling industry. As amazing as it may seem right now, Bedford town once had over three hundred and twenty whalers registered in its fleet, bringing in vast quantities of oil and bone.

"As to what caused the whaling business to fade away from New Bedford and the surrounding ports of New England, you must realize that many factors were involved. First of all, and perhaps most importantly, "rock oil" or petroleum was discovered in 1859 in Pennsylvania. This new discovery dramatically affected the demand for whale oil, as more and more people began to use petroleum and natural gas in place of the expensive oil that came from whales. The second reason centered upon the destruction of large numbers of whaling ships during the War Between the States and in the Arctic Fleet disasters of the 1870s. In just these two instances, well over one hundred whalers were destroyed, causing tremendous financial loss for ship owners.

"To add to the growing problems associated with the business of whaling, it was simply getting more difficult to find whales. Not that whales were totally swept from the seas during the late nineteenth century, but a number of the species of whales were, not withstanding, severely over-hunted. In light of all this, the typical cost of underwriting a whaling voyage became more expensive for the ships had to travel farther, with bigger crews, only to capture a decreasing number of giant mammals.

"The ultimate reason for the shrinking of the whaling industry, however, was the simple fact that people no longer needed whale oil and bone. No profit can come to ship owners if they invest in the procuring of whale products if there is but little demand."

As I finished answering the first lad's questions, another young man in the crowd asked, "Did you ever feel bad about killing whales just to get oil that could have come from someplace else?"

"In the early days of whaling, before the invention of ocean going steamships and powerful cannon-powered whaling guns, I never felt ashamed of my work as a whaler. We were providing a valuable and necessary product for the good of man, without endangering the whale population in any significant way.

"As time passed by, however, I saw first-hand how the glory days of whaling in the era of sailing vessels turned into the impersonal slaughtering of animals that were no longer needed for oil or for much else. The wholesale killing of whales in the sanctuary of the Arctic is a classic example of what has gone wrong with whaling in recent years. As a matter of simple stewardship and common decency, it does not make sense for whales to be hunted to extinction.

"As much as we may deplore the foolish excesses of the whaling industry in the late nineteenth century, these concerns should not be allowed to tarnish the reputations of those men who hunted whales in the early days of sail. After all, such men hunted monsters of the deep, armed only with a simple spear fortified by Yankee courage."

At this point, the crowd that had set itself around my table was fast beginning to disperse. Much to my delight, a number of those in the inn made a point of telling me how grateful they were for the chance to learn the true story of whaling. A feeling of relief soon flooded my soul, as I realized that I had finally told a story that the younger generation needed to hear.

My old friend, Tim Dronner, tipped his hat to the last of the townspeople, and then sat down and said, "Well, my good man, you have gotten something very important off of your chest. Now that the deed is done, what say ye to partaking of one of those bowls of chowder that the proprietor keeps harping about? I've developed a powerful hunger while listening to your chatter."

"Tim, my old friend," I remarked, "now that I have told the story of our lives as whalemen, I may go at any time to meet my Maker in perfect peace. By all means, bring on the chowder, for it is no longer to be feared."

The End

—Bibliography—

Ashley, Clifford W. *The Yankee Whaler*
New York, Houghton Mifflin, 1926.

Ballantyne, R. M. *Fighting the Whales*
New York, 1880.

Block, Irvin.. *The Real Book About Ships*
New York, Garden City Books, 1953.

Burns, Ric. *Into the Deep: America, Whaling & the World*
Arlington, VA, PBS Films –
The American Experience, 2010

Melville, Herman. *Moby Dick*
New York, Harper & Brothers, 1851

Pease, Zephaniah W. *The History of New Bedford*
New York, The Lewis Historical Publishing Company, 1918.

Reinfeld, Fred. *Whales and Whaling*
New York, Garden City Books, 1960.

Sanderson, Ivan T. *Follow the Whale*
Boston, Little Brown, 1956.

Shapiro, Irwin. *The Story of Yankee Whaling*
New York, American Heritage Publishers, 1959.

Whipple, A.B.C. *Yankee Whalers in the South Seas*
New York, Doubleday, 1954.

How To Order GLP Titles

Great Light Publications may be ordered through a number of independent distributors. To obtain a complete listing of distributors who carry some or all of the books published by GLP, please visit our website at: www.greatlightpublications.com

How To Contact GLP

If you wish to become an independent distributor of GLP titles, or if you have general questions or suggestions, please contact:

Great Light Publications
422 S. Williams Ave.
Palatine, IL 60074

Email address: mikem@greatlightpublications.com